ONE FRIDAY IN NAPA

ONE FRIDAY IN NAPA

a novel

JENNIFER HAMM

SHE WRITES PRESS

Published 2023
Printed in the United States of America
Print ISBN: 978-1-64742-529-6
E-ISBN: 978-1-64742-530-2
Library of Congress Control Number: 2023903042

For information, address:
She Writes Press
1569 Solano Ave #546
Berkeley, CA 94707

Interior Design by Tabitha Lahr

She Writes Press is a division of SparkPoint Studio, LLC.

To my mom and dad

chapter one

LOS ANGELES, 1996

The clock on her bedside table read 5:07 a.m. when the phone startled her awake. Vene's cheek was pressed heavily into her pillow. She ran a groggy mental check. She was off work this month, so there could be no baby, no hospital, and no pregnant client needing emergency help. Her husband, Tony, was gently snoring beside her. That left Dani. Could it be Dani? Her eyes snapped open at the thought of her eighteen-year-old daughter, and she snatched at the phone.

"Hello?" she whispered.

"Hello, sweetheart," a man's voice replied.

"Dad? Is that you?" She was relieved, albeit cautious.

"Yes, darling. I'm sorry, did I wake you?"

"No, it's fine. Is everything okay?"

"I wanted to reach you before you went off to work. I don't know your schedule."

"Don't worry. It changes a lot. But it's so early. Why are you up? What's going on?"

He paused. And then with his usual inimitable calm, he said, "It's your mother. She's not well. No need to panic, but it might be a good idea for you to come and visit." He took a deep breath. "Soon."

Adrenaline flooded her body. Adrenaline and fear. Her father had never asked her to come home, and it could only mean one thing. "I'll leave today," she replied quietly.

"Good, good. Thank you, Vene." He sounded anxious. "See you later then."

Vene sat motionless for a moment. She had known this call would come for some time now. That it was no longer an "if" but a "when." Her father hadn't given her any details; she didn't really need them. She would leave and figure out the rest later. Vene, short for Venerdi, which means "Friday" in Italian, is pronounced "Vee-nee." Who knew why that day of the week had been important to her parents. They'd certainly never come up with a good answer when pressed. Shameful as it was, it wasn't panic that made her agree to go so quickly; neither had love played much of a part. She had stayed away when her mother first fell ill, and now too much time had passed for her to justify, however good her reasons might be. She and her mother got on horribly, a fact easier to live with long-distance. The thought of finally going home and confronting that truth made her literally nauseous.

She went into the bathroom and stared into the mirror, examining her face. What new wrinkles in time had made it to her forehead overnight? Had guilt found its way into the furrows between her brows? Wow, she looked old. Her eyes were puffy and red. She thought about her mother's eyes. Big, green, and mysterious, while her own were brown and dull. Take out the windows to the soul, though, and there was more of a resemblance. The wide mouth, full lips. "From the nose down," her dad would say, "you look just like her." Sort of ironic, she thought. As was the fact that she couldn't find a way to love her mother, even while knowing that losing her would be the defining moment of her life.

She started to pack her toiletry bag. Hormone gels, essential medications, black mascara, vitamin D drops, Claritin. The door opened abruptly, and she jumped at the sight of Tony on the threshold, squinting in the bright light.

"Oh my God, you scared me."

"Is someone in labor?" He wiped the sleep from his eyes.

"No, sorry I woke you. Go back to bed."

"I'm up. What's going on?" He was looking at her expectantly, his energy always willing.

"It's my mom," she said. And then, "I think she's dying."

"Oh . . . shit. That's not good."

"I need to go home."

"Of course."

"I don't know for how long. I'm not sure what's happening."

"Go for as long as you need."

"I don't know what I need—I just want to do the right thing, you know?" Suddenly, she felt numb.

"I get it." He touched her hand gently. "You finish packing, I'll go make coffee."

Vene's '96 metallic green Saab had enough room for as many suitcases as she might need, but she stuffed only a few days' worth of clothing and her running shoes into an overnight bag and went downstairs. Tony had an extra-large dark roast waiting for her and a bag of her favorite snacks: customized trail mix with chunks of dried mango, a few small packets of Oreo cookies, a banana, and a big water bottle with lemon slices. The man knew her well.

"Not quite fully committed, I see," he observed, looking at her meager bag.

"Not wanting to go at all," Vene replied honestly.

"It was never going to be easy."

"I just hope she's not in pain."

"All the more reason to go now. Just be with her for a little while."

They looked at each other, realizing that they didn't know what that actually meant. Vene didn't need to tell him to stay back, at least for the moment. He couldn't leave his job for too many days, and anyway, there would come a time when she would need him more. But on top of that, there was always an undercurrent of hesitation about bringing Tony to Napa. Her mother was never gracious to him, and one less conflict between mother and daughter was probably a good thing. So they shared a sweet and lingering kiss that would have to last them, and off she went.

Vene had been raised in Napa, a small town four hundred miles away, clustered in the grape belt of Northern California. She had lived in LA for thirty years since, but Napa would always be home—even though it had been nearly a year since her last visit. There would always be next month, a better time, she had reassured herself. These excuses were her only means of avoiding friction and confrontation with her mother, and soon staying away became the norm. Well, hers, anyway.

It was a long drive but not a difficult one. Once Interstate 5 north was far behind her and she passed the turnoff for Highway 12, she switched off the radio. The weather was her favorite: 60 degrees, crisp, and sunny. She drove the western length of the Silverado Trail with only the sound of the wind blowing. The sunroof was open, and the blue sky above felt like freedom. She paid that bit extra for the sunroof at the dealership just for a day like today. Now it was time to let the landscape, with its trees bent into tunnels, fill her mind. A love of nature was one of her "gifts," her father used to say—her innate understanding of the soil, the weather, the vines. Tuning into the natural world was calming; it made her feel part of something greater. Regardless of the tension that lay in store, Napa was a sacred place for her, and autumn was easily her favorite season in the valley. She took off her Ray-Bans and absorbed the colors. The vines were a tangle of emerald, red, and gold with the grass thick and vibrant beneath them. The grape harvests mostly concluded in October, but it was a local secret that fall was the best time of year for color.

She came to a stop sign and saw a deer eating some grass by the side of the road. She could swear it looked up with its big milky eyes and stared right at her, like it wanted to say, "Welcome home." She caught herself smiling back. As soon as she reached the town of Yountville, she felt the nostalgia. The Winston Family Estate sign that heralded her turnoff was only a few miles farther. Her heart lifted every time she saw that sign; something about the history and sense of belonging was inescapably soothing. She took the right turn hard and fast up the long gravel drive. She loved sliding around the familiar curves of her road, each so intimate from endless childhood bike rides trying to avoid bumps that never got filled. The evening sun flashed its last glory on the tips of the vines beyond the hills. Napa locals were right to be proud—a place didn't get more beautiful than this.

Rising on a gentle slope with commanding views, her family's house was one of the grandest in the valley, a timeless stone fortress covered in ivy, which this time of year turned as gold as the sunset. Built in the late 1800s, the house sat on three hundred acres of fertile land and extended in a U formation over fifteen-thousand square feet overlooking the rows and rows of grapevines crisscrossing the surrounding hills. Two more houses, one for guests and the other for staff, sat on adjacent slopes tucked under a canopy of ancient spreading oak trees. Vene pulled up to her usual spot on the gravel outside the main house where she had parked since she was sixteen. Her father's 1944 green-and-black Rolls-Royce Phantom III was parked beside her. It was always a sight to behold with its statesmanlike curves. Inside it had dark green leather seats and mahogany wood paneling; it was famously the same make and color as the one Churchill rode in during the war—a limited edition. Her father had bought it for her mother as a wedding present, but it was no secret that driving it himself on a Saturday afternoon was his favorite pastime.

She switched off the engine and sank back into the lumbar support of her seat, taking one extra moment to gain her composure before entering the fray. The reality of finally being there was almost paralyzing. Suddenly, she noticed a raindrop on her windshield like a single tear falling from above. Her heart felt tight. The heat of the journey was replaced with a cold slap, and out of nowhere clouds had formed. Wind stirred the air. The inside of the car began to fog, and her hands trembled. She wrapped her scarf around her neck and stared at the tiny Buddha bobblehead that dangled from her mirror. A light turned on outside the front door. "Get out of the car," Vene ordered herself.

She eased her way out and slowly walked up the path, noting the cracks in the old flagstones, their edges crumbling. She looked up and there was Max, standing in the doorway as if he held the house on his shoulders. Strong and stocky, he had to be over eighty years old by now. Maximo, Max, was an Italian immigrant who had lived on the estate longer than he ever lived by the Med, but he still looked like he could have been cast in *Goodfellas* with his heavy features and slicked-back white hair. He had been all things to all of them since she was born: houseman, head chef, chief of staff, and most importantly, guardian of this sanctuary the whole Winston family held dear. It was hard to imagine life here without him. Without Max what remained polished might have been raw with decay.

"Vene, I'm so happy to see you," Max greeted her, opening his arms, something he rarely did for anyone. Vene's eyes instantly flooded. She hugged him back, allowing herself an extra moment in his comforting embrace.

"I can't believe it, Max. I didn't think . . . I didn't know . . ." Her words trailed off until she couldn't find them anymore.

"Come inside. I will get your bags. Your father's in the study."

Vene walked inside and stopped in the entrance hall. They say a house is just walls and that the memories live inside you, but she didn't feel that way. The estate, despite its scale, felt like a safe space where not only all things were possible but where each corner, every room, held a living picture from her childhood. And then there was that smell! Always something mouthwatering. Usually at this time of day it was focaccia. Oh, how she had missed Max's cooking and that feeling she got from the first bite of his magic. Coming home was always a sensory overload, and she hadn't even walked past the entrance hall. She paused at the door of her father's study, aware as always of the inner struggle between the woman she had become and the little girl who had once lived here. The daughter/mother/wife dance, each vying for authority. Who would present after she entered? Silly to have to remind herself of the grown-up she'd become.

She knocked and entered. Small dust particles trickled through the last rays of sunshine from the large bay windows. Her father, Jonathan, now a smaller version of himself at eighty-seven, sat in his big leather armchair reading. It was remarkable how dignified he still appeared, always dressed in his trouser suit pants, pin-striped shirt, and cardigan sweater, ready for whatever formality the day might bring. He barely had any hair left, just a few gray strands on either side of a bald head. His once bright blue eyes now looked tired behind his wireless frames. His face was round and wrinkled, with a pronounced frown line between his eyes that she always imagined had come about from reading and thinking so much. He still had a firm command over the major decisions involving the estate and vineyard, but had long since given up his political career. That decision had given him the gift of time, something that had been in short supply his entire working life.

"Hi, Dad," she said. He looked up from his chair and pushed his glasses higher on his nose.

"Vene," he said with a loving smile. When he did not get up, which said a lot, she bent down next to him and buried her head on his chest. She wrapped her arms around him for a long time and could have cried, but didn't. Her dad was a steady ship, and he allowed her to hold on for as long as she needed. Today, she needed a long time. She finally let go and sat in the chair opposite him.

"What are you reading?" Vene asked.

"Crichton. This chap writes great sci-fi stories. Just love it."

It was definitely a departure from the classics and poetry he used to relish: Hemingway, Wordsworth, Shelley. But at least he was still reading, and that comforted her. She noticed two newspapers, the *Wall Street Journal* and the *New York Times*, spread across the coffee table—again a far cry from the four or five daily papers he used to have. As far back as she could remember, she pictured her father reading. He was the one who read to her at night, he was the one who taught her how to write, and he was the one responsible for her love of poetry. Her mother was the practical one, whereas her father allowed his mind to escape into the intoxicating world of literature whenever he could. A true word merchant, he used to give her extra coins when she was growing up for every word she used over four syllables.

Vene looked out the window. Dusk had settled, and the view disappeared into darkness. She could only just make out the shapes of the big trees in the distance. She felt cold with the onset of night. "So, how's Mom doing?" She reached across to him, noticing how frail his hands looked. Once they had seemed so big to her, but now they appeared almost small in her hands, and covered with age spots, veins, and wrinkles.

He put down his book. He had a diplomat's face, and such a good one that no one other than her and her mother would have guessed he was capable of any emotion at all. He stood up slowly, as though each vertebra had to be stacked perfectly, and then moved to the fireplace, readying the logs to make a fire.

"She's not well." He cleared his throat. "Not well at all, I'm afraid. Doctors can't do anything now. It's just about making sure she's comfortable."

Vene nodded. Wordlessly they crumpled old newspapers that lay next to the logs and together built a tower to ignite into a great fire, a chore from her childhood that he'd taught her to enjoy. So her mother was dying? There was so much to say, and yet she couldn't think of anything. She was sorry she had been away so long, and once again guilt threatened to choke her. She couldn't cry because she couldn't believe it. Not yet.

"How is work? And how's Dani?" her dad asked, putting a match to the wood. She was happy for the question.

"She's loving college, and work is good. Tony is pretty swamped. The advertising industry has never been so busy in LA. Big agencies want to base themselves there as well as New York. He's producing a lot of big budget commercials now. And there's less travel on his end preproduction-wise." She realized she was wittering on and stopped. Her dad had a deferential but blank expression on his face as he watched the flames. She'd explained Tony's job a hundred times, but she still wasn't sure her father knew, or cared particularly, what her husband actually did for a living. "And I'm busier than ever. I've helped with the delivery of eight babies this year alone. I guess word of mouth is finally working for me."

"What is it called again, your service?"

"Doula. I'm a doula. It's a Greek word that means, well, 'female slave,'" she explained, laughing. "Literally."

"Oh," her dad replied politely. Vene had known when she became a doula that there wouldn't be much chat about it with her parents. Deemed way too hippieish, she'd chosen a profession that didn't translate to their generation. At first, they thought she was becoming a midwife, and when she explained that she didn't actually deliver the baby but was there as a birthing coach, she'd sensed their disinterest. She didn't blame them; her peer group had found incredible ways to profit from child-rearing, and this, to her parents, seemed as indulgent as bottle warmers and baby massage. For Vene, though, becoming a doula had been cathartic. Every woman should have someone present whose sole purpose was to provide emotional support and reassurance. The reality of giving birth was the purest experience in the world, equal only to death. She'd given up a pregnancy once—chosen her baby's fate, something she still grappled with. She hadn't had the support she so badly needed then. So yes, being a doula was her small way of making sure that other women didn't have to go through the pain she had, regardless of their circumstances.

She changed the subject. "Dani wants to come up too."

"Good. That's good. Soon, I hope." The mention of Dani always made her father smile. He watched the flames burning through the newspaper until it took the kindling, with a crackle and a pop.

"I'm gonna go up and see Mom. Can I get you anything?" Vene waited for a response, but her father just sat down and picked up his book. He didn't open it, just held it in his lap and stared out the window. She stood watching him. Her strong, wise father whose stature and intellect had always made her feel protected now appeared tired and ever so slightly defeated. She looked out the window too, suddenly feeling lost in the past. They had solved so many world problems in this room. Every history lesson she'd ever studied, every English essay she'd ever written had started with one of her father's stories. Their discussions often led to debates, which she would always lose—not from lack of trying but because of his forensic knowledge of history. "It's all in the details," he'd say. "Look closer . . . think!" She loved that room; it was calm and still and held a lifetime of memories for her.

Upstairs, she stood outside her parents' bedroom door. She couldn't hear anything coming from inside. It was surreal to be there at that moment waiting to open the door to see her mother, for what could be one of the last times. It was too much to comprehend. Cancer was the villain and the fight had begun a while ago, but she always thought her mother would emerge the victor. On her last visit here, her mother had been full of life, running the annual Napa Valley fundraiser for the children's hospital. They'd argued and she'd left angry, thinking she'd punish her mother by staying away. She promised herself she wouldn't call for at least a month, long enough for her mother to surely notice. But had she? It was hard to know. One month turned into two, and two into six, with only the odd random phone call in between. This was definitely a forced reentry, and once again Vene had to work out what to do with her anger, not just from their last encounter but from years of it.

Max came up the stairs. He put his hand on her shoulder, and she could feel his understanding in the simple gesture. She already felt emotionally raw and hadn't even entered the room. With a soft knock, he opened the door for her, and then tactfully withdrew. She stepped inside and paused. Her mother lay in bed with the covers pulled all the way up. Her perfect oval face peeked out over the top, and her almond-shaped green eyes were closed. Her hair, now a patchy gray, was pinned back into a loose bun. The first thing Vene wondered was when her mother had given up coloring her hair dark brown. But then she noticed the metal table at her mother's bedside with various machines and a tall pole extending upwards holding a drip. An irritating beeping noise came from a heart monitor. Vene's eyes took in the reality of what "now" looked like. She approached the bed and kissed her mother's cheek softly, noting that she still smelled the same, Chanel No. 5; that familiar fragrance invited an odd relief.

"That beeping sound makes me want to throw that machine out the window," her mother said in a croaky voice. She opened her eyes slowly and looked at her daughter.

"How did you know I was thinking that?" Vene asked, startled.

"Same as hide-and-go-seek."

Yes, that was true. Her childhood consisted of game after game of hide-and-go-seek, and since Vene didn't have any siblings, it was either her mother or poor Max who had to play—and her mother always knew where to look. A wondrous connection Vene thought they had back then. Vene liked to hide, and her mother, she thought, liked to find her.

She wanted to pull up a chair and sit close to the bed, but she hesitated. It was awkward with all the plugs and cords and tubes. Given her doula work, she was used to hospitals and bedside manners, but this was different. This was her mother. The caretaker inside of her shriveled. *Go slow*, she thought. *Move closer to the bed and see if she flinches.* The metal table had wheels on it and so she carefully moved it backwards, failing to notice the cord connecting the monitor. *Beeeeeep!* The machine went nuts.

"Oh no, what happened, what did I do? I'm so sorry!"

"Sounds like someone died," her mother joked dryly. The nurse hurried into the room and expertly plugged all the wires back into the machine. Vene looked on, feeling terrible. "Kelly, this is my daughter, Vene," Olivia said to the nurse.

"It's just the monitor. Don't worry," Kelly said, seeing Vene's expression.

"Why does she have a drip? I mean, I know why she would have one, but are medicines being pumped in? She can still eat, right?" Vene's questions shot out one after the other.

"Your mother was quite dehydrated when I got here a few days ago, so she had to go on a drip to sort that. She's better now, but we keep it there just in case."

"Just in case?" Vene questioned.

"Just in case I'm not feeling well again," Olivia interjected.

"Oh, right," Vene said. "Of course."

"Nice to meet you, finally," the nurse said to Vene, extending her hand.

The remark had been innocent, but shame flooded Vene's heart. *Finally. Final.* She shook Kelly's hand. The nurse had a kind smile, almost apologetic for meeting under those circumstances. Vene watched her as she held her mother's shoulders forward and gently maneuvered her in order to fluff the pillows behind her head. All she could think of was how her mother must have hated being touched. She just wasn't the sort of person who was open to being handled. By anyone. Let alone a stranger. For the nurse, it must have been difficult too. Palliative care for a dying woman who needed more help than she was comfortable accepting. Her mother's body looked frail and small. Vene had been four inches taller than her since her freshman year of high school, but it had never been her mother's physical body that made her feel so powerful. There was a little bit more fussing, and then the nurse left.

"How come you didn't call? I would have come sooner had I known," Vene said quietly. *Months sooner?*

"We spoke on the phone."

"Yes, Mom, we did, but I would have come had I known . . ."

"You cut your hair," Olivia interrupted.

"Yes," Vene said, self-consciously putting a strand behind her ear, as though to hide it from her mother's critical eye.

"Pity. You have such lovely hair. Not many people can wear their hair long."

"Yes, well, I thought I'd try something new. It's just a few layers."

"Oh."

"It will grow back," Vene said, shifting uneasily under her mother's scrutiny. "Anyway . . . you were explaining how you are feeling?"

"The doctors tell you so many things. I only just started to feel unwell last month and wasn't due for another check for some time, but your father made me go and see someone. I was sure he was wrong, that it hadn't come back. But by then it was, well, it was . . ." She motioned her hands dismissively over her whole body, as if each and every part of herself was an unwanted pest. Vene watched her lying in the bed with just the sound of the annoying monitor for a little while longer. Silence had never been an easy thing between them. It always felt like a void more than a peaceful quiet. They'd had enough acrimony and confrontation, and now their relationship consisted only of banal, superficial discussions rather than anything worthwhile. Vene rarely challenged her mother anymore, and it seemed a terrible time to start again.

"Are you comfortable?" she asked eventually. "Can I get you anything?"

"I'm fine," Olivia replied, closing down any opportunity for her to help.

"Are you sure?" Vene pressed. "I can go downstairs and make you some hot water and lemon, or a ginger brew of some sort? I saw Max; he's making focaccia and it smells amazing. He's always making the house smell so good with his cooking. Last time I was here he made that incredible *parmigiana di melanzane* that Tony said was the best he ever had." The minute she said Tony's name, she regretted it.

"When was that?"

Nope—her mother didn't miss a beat. "The holidays, just before Christmas, remember?" Vene replied, hoping there was an off chance her mother had forgotten.

"Oh, yes. Christmas." Her tone implied she hadn't forgotten anything.

Again, acrimony. Vene stared at her mother's face, her lips pressed firmly together. Last Christmas had gone so poorly that she and Tony had left before the New Year's Eve party. How could she have stayed when her mother all but dismissed her entire marriage? Having spent years trying to foster a relationship between her husband and her mother, Vene was exhausted by the whole thing and beyond frustrated.

"I saw Dad briefly downstairs. He's reading a Crichton novel. He looks like he's doing okay."

Her mother didn't respond.

"How's he holding up?"

"Your father's a rock, always a rock, but he's older," her mother replied curtly. It was true. Vene had seen it immediately. Even when she'd been a wayward teenager, her father had always been the one to weigh in with a nod or a quiet word. His innate trust and understanding of her remained a huge comfort. Now he was the one who was going to need some looking after, and the thought made her unaccountably sad.

"But he looks well, considering."

"You're not here. You can't see much in a short visit," her mother said matter-of-factly.

Anger, even a tinge of hatred flooded through Vene. She flushed. Ten minutes in her mother's company. That's all it took. There was no running away this time, and she felt instantly claustrophobic. Her mother responded by pulling the sheets up above her chest and closing her eyes. The room went still like a dramatic pause awaiting the next moment. Vene raked her cuticles against the fabric of her sweater—a habit of hers from childhood that took her mind off of what was in front of her. She sat stiffly, watching her mother, waiting to see if she was sleeping or just resting. The beeping from the machine continued. How close life was to death. A single beep, then one long continuous alarm as a person crashed into darkness. How much easier would it be when that happened? To never again have to figure out the right thing to say or do. To never again feel as though she always got it wrong. There was no escaping the chasm between them, and the hardest part was the "why"—why had she felt distanced from her own mother her whole life? Why didn't her mother like her?

NAPA, 1946

Fall menu for a dinner party—tried and true
Start with the duck hors d'oeuvres and pâté
Minestrone alla Napoletana
Spaghetti all'amatriciana
Osso buco alla Milanese
Profiteroles

The doorbell rang with the first of their guests. Olivia sat upstairs on the edge of her bed in her undergarments. Early on in her marriage, the role of hostess came easily to her—but the desire to be on display did not. She was a beautiful woman who garnered attention from men, with or without her consent. On a good day, she effortlessly put on a dress, pinning her hair up loosely so that a few curls fell down over her pronounced cheekbones. On a good day, she almost danced amongst the guests. She could fill the room with her elegance, grace, and smile. She knew Jonathan loved their dinner parties, and aware they were her duty, she did her best to please him. But on a bad day, all she could think about was how her longing to have a child had broken her spirit. She felt as though there was nothing female about her at all. On a bad day, sadness tore away at her moment by moment. She spent too many hours in bed, and with Jonathan traveling so often, she wasn't even sure how much he noticed. It seemed like every woman she knew except her was pregnant almost as a result of the war, but for Olivia, the war had become the excuse she relied upon. It had been the war, not her barren body, that had prevented her from conceiving.

And it wasn't just her. Jonathan was also wound tightly. Traveling to Washington, Quebec, Cairo, all for diplomatic conferences on behalf of President Truman was stressful and exhausting. It was often difficult to communicate with him about personal issues when he got home and even more impossible to find time to be intimate. He saw their relocation to Napa Valley as a safe haven away from the climate of fear and destruction that had gripped the nation during the war. Olivia was unwilling to shatter his illusion. Her fears of never having a family remained her own quiet nightmare. These thoughts always came when the dress lay on the chair beside her, and the last thing she felt like was being a good hostess.

"Olivia, darling, our guests are arriving!" yelled Jonathan with excitement from downstairs. It was her signal to come. Make a dramatic entrance down the spiral stairwell to create the perfect hospitable welcoming. She reached automatically for her black Dior dress, the safe choice, and put it on. It had a long billowy skirt with pleats, soft rounded shoulders, and a narrow waist that showed off her figure well. Without any more effort, she looked beautiful, and she willed herself out of the room and down the stairs.

The Winston family kitchen had always been the center of energy in the house. It was a cook's kitchen with two ovens, two sinks, and a scullery at the side. A huge central butcher's block housed one of the ovens and provided ample space for chopping and displaying fruit bowls and baked goods. This was Max's domain and where he could always be found, baking, preparing, tasting the food. Max embodied a professional chef without the clichéd prima donna temperament. He loved food as much as he loved the Winstons, with a belly as big as his heart.

Tonight was a particularly busy evening on the estate, and the entire staff had been called upon to help. Olivia and Jonathan were entertaining *the* luminary winemakers and wine producers with the hopes of impressing them: Fernande de Latour of

Beaulieu Vineyard, Felix Salmina of Larkmead, Charles Forni of the Napa Valley Co-op, Robert Mondavi of CK Mondavi and Sons, John Daniel Jr. of Inglenook, Louis M. Martini, and Louis Stralla. These men had formed an official trade group a few years back in 1944 called the Napa Valley Vintners. Together they dealt with the problems of price control, shortage of labor, bottles, and railcars for eastern shipments of wine, and exchanged ideas of how to put Napa Valley wine on the global map. If the Winston family were to produce quality wine here, joining these vintners would give status to the label and help marketing and trade. These dinners were the most glamorous the valley had ever seen. Only the best of Jonathan's wine collection was ever served, and the food was always paired to perfection.

Tonight was no exception. Taken from his Italian collection of Chianti, the sangiovese grapes were chosen for their aroma of cherries and violets that balanced the palate superbly. Max went into the dining room to recheck that the glasses had been laid correctly, never trusting those details to any other staff member. He ran a tight kitchen and was a perfectionist about presentation. By the time Olivia entered the kitchen, Max was plating the first course of soup. Next door in the dining room, guests were already seated and chatting away. She instructed the staff to start taking out the soups, quickly dipping a spoon into one of the bowls to taste it first.

"Excellent flavors, Max, slightly different this time. Thicker, and . . ."

"I used cavolo nero with a hint of thyme," Max replied.

"Last time we didn't use any fresh herbs. Interesting." Olivia grabbed the open cookbook called *Il talismano della felicità*, the talisman of happiness, and wrote a few notes in the margin. The book was Max's mother's copy brought with him from Italy, and in a touching gesture he had given it to Olivia shortly after her arrival on the estate. It was written in Italian, and although Olivia had muttered about an English translation, Max was adamant that she understand Italian cooking through Italian eyes and words. His tuition had begun during one of Jonathan's long overseas trips away. Jonathan would have never approved of her involvement in the kitchen. He would not have considered it the proper place for a diplomat's wife, so her interest in food was always kept from him. Olivia's fascination with what Max intended to plant on the estate had ignited their first culinary discussion, and their friendship had grown from there. Both seemed to find refuge in the other, and although he was considered staff and she was the lady of the house, cooking became their equalizer. She put her spoon in the sink and with a quick fix of her hair left the kitchen for the dining room.

chapter two

1996

The house was quiet. Vene sat in bed staring out her window facing the rising sun. She felt raw. Though always within arm's reach, sleep had evaded her most of the night. She was exhausted but was trained to get up. It was funny to her how little things had changed in her room since she was a girl. Framed pictures from her teenage years, parties, and award ceremonies still on the shelves. Trophies won for horseback riding and swimming, two sports long since abandoned. Her small enamel Halcyon Days box collection was balanced on glass shelving next to Lalique crystal perfume bottles from France. A toy replica of a London bus and Big Ben, showing off early travels, sat next to a small teddy bear tucked away into one of the corners. If her room was any indication, then with the exception of a small framed picture of Dani, it looked as though she hadn't grown up past the age of thirteen. Perhaps her mother felt more comfortable this way.

She chose not to shower for fear the noise of the pipes would wake her sleeping mother. Wake her mother . . . oh, the years spent trying not to wake her mother! The intricate comings and goings in this big house, bypassing creaking floorboards and squeezing through nearly shut doors. They came down on the opposite sides of so many things—*don't wear that, don't go there, try that, have that, use that, be this but not that . . .* the list went on and on. Her mother had a deep fear of things breaking or getting ruined. Life for her was calculated and specific, polished and poised. It was all about boundaries and curfews, and none of it involved black eyeliner. Vene's desire to grab a hold of everything, toss it into the air, and see where it came down had made her childhood a combat zone. Most discussions turned to arguments, the types with slammed doors and broken hinges. Eventually their collective resentments piled up so high there was no room left to store them in. She didn't need her mother in the traditional sense and had pushed her away long before she, herself, understood why. Vene had a crazy independence early on, which seemed to infuriate her mother. In turn, her mother was distant, and her version of being involved resulted in telling Vene what to do. To Vene it always felt as though her mother resented her choices, and that became exhausting. She often wondered what made her mother that way—her own life had always seemed to fall into place quite easily and naturally. So why all the rules? Surely she saw enough of herself in her daughter, Vene thought for the umpteenth time, to know that she too would survive.

She went downstairs to the kitchen, the smell of baking greeting her before she even opened the door. "Good morning, Vene. Croissants should be ready in a few minutes," Max said. *Oh, thank God for Max,* she thought almost tearfully.

"Morning, Max. Just you and me this early, like always."

The kitchen unfailingly looked like it had just been cleaned, a rule Max adhered to regardless of what was going on or how many people he was cooking for. She admired his professionalism, as it would have been very easy to slack off when it was just her parents in the house, especially with her mother upstairs the whole time and Max getting on in years.

"Actually, your father's up too. He went out with the groundskeeper for an early walk to check on the vines."

"That's strange. Has he been getting up earlier lately?"

"I think he's having a difficult time sleeping as well."

"I see." She had noticed that her dad had taken up residence in the guest bedroom nearest the master, his books on the bedside table, his favorite antique alarm clock perched on top of them. Max busied himself around the kitchen, opening up the fridge and bringing out various fruits and yogurts. He readied a tray with cutlery, plates, and glasses. His hands were still agile and strong and he moved about without any noticeable pain, but she could smell the ointment he must have rubbed on his joints, Tiger Balm or something equally therapeutic. She watched him for a little while.

"Shall I make some coffee? I think I saw some dark roast beans in the pantry last night."

"Yes. There's a fresh pack behind the filters on the second shelf."

The walk-in pantry was one of her favorite spaces in the entire house. It had a wraparound counter with shelves above and storage below. As a child she used to hide herself away in there with friends, gossiping and eating cookies from the jars, finding all the random treats Max had so carefully hidden in the cupboards. She was pretty sure he knew she emptied them, as the jars were miraculously filled up each week, but he never mentioned it. She jumped up onto the counter and looked up at the shelves. They were so perfectly organized: flour and sugar, baking items all to the left; cereals, snacks, canned food in the middle; household goods to the right. Once, she had tried to replicate this pantry in her own home; it had lasted until the moth infestation destroyed everything and all the food had to be thrown away. She'd lost the will for order after that but had to admit there was also something really nice about matching Tupperware and labeled glass jars filled neatly to the top.

She found the coffee on the second shelf, next to the filters, just as Max said. She noticed several old books stored there too and took them down. One in particular, *Il talismano della felicità*, was big and worn. It looked inviting, so she took it back with her into the kitchen.

"I didn't know you used cookbooks, Max. This one looks like you spilled a hundred dinners all over it," she joked. She opened a random page. "Let's see . . . osso buco alla Milanese . . . When did you last cook this?" Max looked over and shrugged. "I'm learning a bit of Italian now," she said idly.

"Oh?" he said.

"Tony is teaching me, and I just started a class. It's only once a week, but hey . . . *Sciogliere il burro in una padella larga* . . ." she read tentatively. "See, I can read it okay, but Lord knows what I've just said!"

"You told me to kill a small cow."

"Really?"

Max went back to sorting berries on a plate. He had a way of paying attention without ever seeming like he was pressing for more. It made him the perfect person to confide in and, if she was honest, the only member of the family willing to discuss her second husband.

"Tony would have come, you know. To the house. But I didn't know what to expect, and Mom made it pretty crystal last time that she's beyond not interested in him, so . . ."

"Your mother is not perfect, but she loves you. Loves Daniela," he said matter-of-factly, slicing an apple.

"Yeah, well, that much I figured out." She looked casually through the cookbook as they spoke. Dani's father, Robert, was the son of another Napa family now living in LA, and a man her mother seemed to adore for no apparent good reason. Vene had been so desperate for her mother's approval in her younger years that she'd gone as far as marrying Robert just to please her. It hadn't been a conscious decision, but certainly must have reflected a sick, subconscious one. At least that was the conclusion she'd arrived at a few years back after a lot of expensive analysis. "This book is pretty torn up, Max. And old. You wrote all of these markings? Funny you chose English and not Italian."

"Ah . . ." He hesitated. "Those aren't mine."

"Whose are they?" She flipped the pages back and forth. "It looks like . . ." She tried to decipher the handwriting.

Max paused. He looked at her for a moment before answering. "They're your mother's," he finally replied.

"My mother's?" The idea startled her. "Huh. Well, yes, now that you've said it, I can see it is her writing. But that makes no sense. Why did she write in your cookbook?"

"I gave it to her—it was hers to write in. She took lots of notes. Not just in there. They're everywhere in this kitchen," he explained with a quick gesture of his hand.

"But she hates to cook. She never cooked before. When did she start? When I left for college?"

"Oh, about fifty years ago . . . give or take," Max said, averting his eyes.

"Fifty years?!" She shook her head incredulously. That didn't fit at all with her recollection of the way things had been.

Vene began furiously turning the pages, one after the other, finding notes and markings on almost every one. Had her mother really made all these dishes? It would have taken her months to get through the entrées alone. She tried to think back to a day when she remembered her cooking. Her whole childhood it had been Max in the kitchen, and her mother—well yes, at times nearby, fussing, perhaps tasting, laying napkins or wine glasses, but certainly never cooking. Even when her father was traveling, Vene had never seen her bake anything, let alone cook a whole meal. She hated it. It was Max who'd taught Vene how to fry an egg, make Bolognese, bake a cake. All the good Italian basics she'd left home with came from him. And her father had enjoyed teaching her how to make an omelet—the only thing he ever did well in the kitchen—but her mother? Never. Nothing. Ever.

"I don't understand . . ." she said, perplexed. "We lived in London till I was nearly ten, and Nanny Kate did all of the cooking. Then we moved here, and you did everything, right? I mean, yeah, I thought it was totally strange how dismissive she was of anything to do with the kitchen, but it was the wine that interested her, wasn't it? The obsession about the vineyard and the gardens. Even now . . ."

Max continued to set up the tray in front of him. "She was passionate about food, a perfectionist. It took a lot of time and a lot of recipes to get her to relax and stop with her head."

"Are you serious, Max?"

"She didn't really cook after you were born. But before then, she was very good. She could have been a chef. Of course, it wasn't something she discussed or did out in the open. An American diplomat's wife was not meant to be in the kitchen back then."

"So she had to secretly cook? With you? Wow, that's crazy. I just can't imagine it. If she loved it so much, why would she just stop? Did my father make her?"

Max stood still, as though lost in the past. "She was happy cooking," he said. "That's all I know for sure."

1946

Menu for his homecoming—favorites!

Tartine di fegato di pollo

Ravioli di ricotta

Baccala

Tiramisu

"Ouch! Holy horsefeathers, that hurts!" Olivia yelped, sucking her finger. "Max, quick, get me a Band-Aid." Blood started pouring over the anchovy she'd been chopping.

"The innards are meant to come out when you pull the head. Never try and cut them out first—it's very messy," Max said calmly, handing her a towel. "Snap the backbones just behind the head with your finger, then pull the head, and it all should come out in one."

"So much effort for such a little fish. I don't even like anchovies."

"Their flavor and natural oils blend well with other fish and sauces. You'll see."

"It's the smell. And they taste like they smell. Yuck. We could have chosen something else from the cookbook, no?" Olivia scrunched up her face.

"This entire menu has come from the estate,—the anchovies from the nearby coast," Max said sternly. "My mother always cooked what was fresh in front of her, never needing to wonder what recipes to follow. It was always a matter of what was ready to pick, to hunt, to fish. Today we caught many anchovies on the net, so tonight it's white perch from the sea with anchovies, and first we will have mushroom soup, followed by asparagus risotto."

Olivia kept working away at the anchovies, humming to herself. "Table for two tonight. Food for an army." She laughed. "Jonathan sure is missing out. Bet you they don't have *pesce persico alle acciughe* in Moscow."

Jonathan had been away for nearly a month this time. His job had gone from full-time to ridiculous, endless hours and commitment. Postwar America was a time of high economic growth and general prosperity but also a time of confrontation. America was at its core a capitalist nation, and together with its allies it stood politically opposed to the Soviet Union and other communist countries. Jonathan's role as a key diplomat had shifted to figuring out this complicated relationship, negotiating and securing US deals abroad. For many Americans, for many of their friends, their lives were about looking forward with rising wages and a general sense of optimism. But for Olivia, there was no escaping the lack of bloom in her world.

A future alone with Jonathan without children felt almost loathsome—a private thought that often scared her and so consequently she buried it. She knew Jonathan wanted a child, and at twenty-six, her days felt numbered. It was his rite and her role. Her doctor couldn't find anything wrong with her and had started to suggest that her state of mind was the cause of her problems, insinuating she was no longer an unwitting victim but in fact a culprit of her condition. Who's to say that wasn't true. And so cooking slowly became a way to express herself, a language of sorts, something positive to focus on. She spent time planting and picking, exploring all the integral flavors of each herb, vegetable, meat. She wanted to know how to mix flavors, experiment with recipes and work out why certain combinations blended well and others didn't. She and Max spent hours cooking together. It was terribly old-fashioned of Jonathan, she thought, not to approve of her being in the kitchen. Status shouldn't matter, and surely not in Napa of all places. But approve he did not, and he'd made that absolutely clear.

He had arrived home from a long trip away. She knew he'd had a difficult time in his negotiations—that he felt exhausted and a bit low. She had prepared perfectly for his homecoming: a hot Epsom salt bath, a gusty fire in his study, and a beautiful new whiskey bought that day from a local distillery. She'd planned to surprise him with all his favorite dishes: chicken liver canapés, ravioli with ricotta cheese, and salted cod. She had put an enormous amount of time, effort, and actual love into the meal, wanting him to not just taste all the flavors but appreciate them too. As they sat at the table, she talked him through the details of each dish, describing how she made it. The freshly picked vegetables she had grown herself, the herbs she'd used and why. At first, she'd been so caught up in her own excitement that she hadn't noticed his less than enthusiastic responses, the way he pushed his fork around the plate with a total lack of interest in the food or the specifics of the menu. Finally, he looked up at her.

"My mother, and her mother before her, never entered the kitchen to cook. That is what staff are for. Max is a perfectly capable chef, and the idea that you would waste your time helping him is pointless. You have plenty to do on the estate," he continued, "especially during my absence. It is a working vineyard, after all."

Olivia had been too shocked to respond. Jonathan seemed to take this as acquiescence. "And as my wife," he reiterated heavily, "you should focus on more valuable ambitions. Surely I have provided enough for you to be able to have freedoms that not every woman is lucky enough to enjoy?"

Deep down, Olivia knew he wasn't being intentionally callous, that this was his way of being supportive. Nevertheless, she didn't know what hurt more: his lack of curiosity in her newly discovered passion or the reality that she was married to a man who didn't understand her at all. It had not occurred to her five years prior to look at Jonathan through any other lens than that of a provider and future father of her children—a man of integrity, strength of character, and worldliness. He was as handsome as she was beautiful. They were well suited and both families had felt proud. But had he ever really "seen" her? Had they ever really been in love? There had always been a strange disconnect in their marriage—a truth she circumvented figuring a baby would fill the void. Fill in the loneliness. A baby would make sense of her life. But in the meantime, cooking was the first thing, the only thing, she turned to every time he left. It had become the only way of creating sustenance for herself. And all he could say was pass the salt.

chapter three

1996

The fall mornings were glorious. Usually a transparent mist hovered over the valley, setting an atmosphere of anticipation and mystery before the sun slowly pushed its way through, lighting up the edges of soft clouds as it did so. While below, the vines rotated in color—red, gold, orange, and green.

Vene took an early walk. Normally she would go for long runs around the property or into town and back, but this morning she was more interested in seeing the vines. She had missed the season's planting, but at least she had made it in time for the end of the harvest. The workers, having begun before sunrise, were finishing their shift. They moved in pairs along each vine, keeping pace with one another, meticulously choosing the best grapes to cut. Each partner, in their large straw hats and muddy boots, stood on opposite sides of the vine, one slightly ahead to reduce the risk of their fingers getting cut. They carried wooden crates to hold the bunches, and once they were full a carrier deposited them in the tractor, then brought back the empty crate. It was backbreaking work, but picking had been her favorite part of the harvest growing up and she knew most of the laborers by name. Many had been with her family for years, some decades.

"*Hola, Pedro. Que tal*?" she said, stopping. Pedro was the vineyard manager in charge of all the workers during harvesting and an incredibly knowledgeable man.

"*Hola, señora*," he replied with a quick knowing smile.

From the looks of it, it was going to be a good year for wine. She broke off a cluster of grapes and inspected it, smelling the beautifully round purple goodness before tossing it into the bin. "*Huele bien*."

"*Sí, esperemos*." He nodded. All the workers hoped for each crop to be the best yet. They felt a collective sense of pride when presented with several bottles of wine for their families at the end of each year. She thrust her hands into the soil and smelled them too. There was a distinct scent, even in the dirt, a hint of blossoms, pungent and fruity. She pulled a purple needle-nose weed from the ground. It was indigenous to Napa and especially to their property. It was a bit of a nuisance plant, but it had a beautiful deep-purple flower that she had always loved. She put the stem in her pocket and grabbed a pair of cutters and gloves from the bin and joined in the final hour of picking.

There was a reason for the valley's success with grapes. As Pedro had explained countless times, in geological terms, California was a brand-new area. It had been created from tectonic plates 150 million years ago when the ocean floor pushed up against the volcanoes and the valleys were formed and carved, mixing up a soup of bedrock material. After millions of years of exposure, it created the diverse soil types found in Napa. This was why so many different varietals grew in the valley—50 percent of the world's soil orders were found there. Winemakers from around the world were envious of Napa's soil quality. From the time their family bought that land the estate had grown grapes, which wasn't always the case on those hills. They were fortunate to have inherited the permitting to harvest grapes—which is rare and therefore doubled their land value. Several land acts had been put into place to protect and conserve the area from urbanization and tourism, and the city council had gone to great lengths to restrict landowners from growing grapes. And they were lucky as well that the cabernet grape, the valley's most illustrious and profitable type, also grew right there.

So much of Vene's upbringing had been about the rhythm of the harvest. It was imperative that each season brought a crop of great quality and quantity to make enough Winston Family cases. They might have been a small label, unlike their neighbors the Mondavis, who'd helped define the area, but they'd still been there since Napa found its way onto the global map as a first-class winemaking region. They remained a modest label mainly because no one in the greater Winston family had the desire to expand, including her father. Jonathan acted more as a figurehead and purveyor of the big picture, leaving the running of the vineyard to his winemaker. And he was known for choosing excellent winemakers. These were the people who were the true craftsmen. They directed the growth and harvest of the grapes, oversaw the crushing and fermentation, and ensured the quality in the aging, blending, and bottling of the wine. Winemaking was more than just a job; it was an art form. The valley was full of families, people living out their dreams—often fantasies—trying to make wine. The underlying characteristic they all shared was passion. Everyone had to be at least a little bit obsessed.

Vene was no different from her father. She loved everything about winemaking but didn't want it to be her life. It was a shame because she'd always thought she had a mind for business and a heart for the land. *It needs to be a calling*, her dad would tell her, and her calling it was not. There was no way around having to settle there, and ultimately she felt restless in Napa.

It was still early morning when she finished her work and walked into the kitchen to get some breakfast. Max was putting her mother's tray together. She noticed the big yellow sunflower placed in the middle and the best silverware wrapped in fresh linen.

"I'll take it up to her, Max."

"What about you, do you want something?"

"Sure. How about a banana and some coffee?"

Max added a banana, coffee, and another fresh croissant onto the tray.

"Thanks. Never going to lose weight around your baking, that's for sure," she said, heading upstairs.

Her mother's door was shut, as always. This time another nurse was outside in the hall, presumably having just begun her shift. There were two nurses who traded off so that she had care 24/7. The nurse knocked, then slowly pushed the door open. Vene thought it respectful considering she knew that her mother had neither the voice nor the energy to stop someone from entering. She went over to the bed and waited a minute, the tray still in her hands. Olivia's eyes were closed, and she wasn't moving at all. If it weren't for the heart monitor, Vene might have thought she was dead. It was a strangely eerie feeling. The nurse signaled for her to leave the tray on the table nearby, and as she did the cups rattled and her mother's eyes opened.

"Sorry, Mom. Didn't mean to wake you."

"You didn't. I wasn't really sleeping. You can't really sleep with all the fussing." She managed to look accusingly at the nurse.

"We have to take some vitals throughout the night. Less than we would at a hospital, so that's good, but it's important to not let things go for too long of a stretch," the nurse explained politely.

"Hmmph," Olivia said.

The nurse busied herself with a printed reading from the machine, checked her mother's pulse, then left. Vene helped her mother sit up a bit better and then placed the tray on the bed in front of her. She poured out coffee for two and sat on the chair opposite. It was stiff and wooden, and she thought that she might switch it out or add pillows a bit later if her mother didn't mind.

"I went picking this morning. Saw Pedro. The grapes were looking so succulent and colorful. Their smell was so sweet. It was really good to be back in the vineyard."

"It was a warm start to the season," Olivia spoke slowly. "The soil was dry. Triggered the buds to break early. Everything bloomed in the beginning of May."

"Oh yes, I think I remember hearing about that."

"Everyone prayed for a mild summer. At least those prayers were answered . . ." Her mother's voice trailed off.

"I'm sorry, Mom."

Ignoring this, Olivia continued, "In any event, there was a good amount of time for the grapes to hang for optimal maturity. The character and flavors should be excellent. You must drink this vintage in a few years' time knowing it's one of the best I have ever seen."

And she meant it. But Vene was suddenly chilled. Her mother's last vintage. Vene wasn't searching for more in this moment; she was holding on to life with her mother in it. She didn't know what to say. Mustn't comment about her dying; mustn't be too emotional. She drank more coffee and let the silence hang between them for a while as they picked at their croissants without appetite. She was amazed by her mother's knowledge of winemaking, particularly about the actual grapes and blending of them. As far as she knew, her mother had never been involved with anything other than the business side of the label, marketing and distribution. But how silly of her not to have assumed that her mother possessed a deep knowledge of what they were selling all those years. And then all the cooking? She had underestimated her mother, clearly. It was like a Polaroid image slowly revealing itself. What would the full picture be, she wondered, when and if it finally came?

"I spoke to Dani," Vene said. Conversations always became easier when they spoke about Dani. "She's planning on coming up here to see you this weekend. I told her no friends, you know.

She still sees that boy from St. Helena every once in a while. He's actually very sweet and comes down to LA. His name is Joe, or something like that." She knew she was beginning to ramble but couldn't stop. "Joe, Joey . . . no, Josh. I don't think they're going out per se, but she's definitely keen. She knew his younger brother growing up. Anyway, I made sure she knew to keep things quiet in the hou—"

"Vene," her mother interrupted with a wave of her hand. "I want to see Dani, and I don't mind her boyfriend being here."

"Mom, he's not her boyfriend—and since when did you become so easygoing about teenage dating, anyway?" This came out unexpectedly harshly. Her eighteen-year-old self instantly riled.

"I want to see her, that's all."

"And she wants to come."

"Good."

"Good," Vene repeated, not knowing what else to talk about.

Olivia began combining the breakfast that Max had served in small containers: yogurt, berries, granola, and seeds, layering them like a beautiful parfait. Even though she'd probably only manage a bite, that the food looked a certain way was clearly important to her. Vene had always thought her mother was too particular, not wanting anyone else to mix or touch her food. And now she wondered if it was the chef in her objecting? There remained so much she didn't understand about her, and time was ticking too quickly for the reconciliation she always thought they'd have. How could it be that as a grown woman she still needed her mother's approval, understanding, and support for her decisions? Her head was screaming. *Why can't I let this shit go?*

She remembered when she was a senior in high school and went shopping for her prom dress with her own money she'd saved up from working at the café in town. She drove all the way to the stores in San Francisco. She must have made a million cappuccinos to pay for that dress. And the truth was, she really wanted her mom to like it. But she should have known. Her mother always had the same look on her face whenever Vene tried anything on. An incredulous "what the hell are you wearing" look. Vene thought it would be different that time because *that* time it was her prom dress. And she was right. It was. That time her mother not only looked at her with distaste but told her she hated it as well. "It is my duty," she'd said, "to be honest." *No,* Vene remembered thinking, *it's not your duty to be honest; it's your duty sometimes to lie just a little bit to make your daughter feel better about herself.* At eighteen, her self-confidence could be determined by something as little as a good dress. *Small moments matter, Mom, they just do.* She felt like shouting at her mother, but instead she poured herself yet more coffee and quietly polished off her croissant.

1946

The master bedroom had one large en suite bathroom with two enclosed toilets on either side—a his and a hers. There were two dressing rooms with their own separate entrances so you didn't have to go through one to get to the other. Olivia's quarters had tulip wallpaper and plush, off-white wool carpet. There was enough storage space for most of her clothes to fit, even though the house had been built in the nineteenth century and without the foresight of walk-in closets. Jonathan's dressing room had dark wooden floorboards and simple walls and could even fit a small leather chair that he liked to sit in while lacing up his shoes. They both firmly believed that one secret to a successful marriage was separate dressing rooms, often getting ready for the day or night without speaking to each other. One evening, however, Jonathan walked into her dressing room.

"Can we talk?"

Olivia was already dressed and sitting in front of her mirror struggling with her pearl necklace. "What is it?"

Jonathan moved behind her, took the necklace, and slowly hooked the clasp. She looked at him through the mirror, realizing how much she needed his soft touch, his attention. He smiled back at her. "What did the doctor say? You went today, yes?"

"Yes," she said, shifting her eyes away.

"I would have gone with you. You didn't have to go alone."

"I know, I know. But it was unnecessary for you to change things." She got up and started rummaging through her jewelry drawer for some earrings.

"So, what did he say?"

"Nothing. And everything. And I'm not pregnant. Well, it's not a hundred percent, but a missed cycle without any other symptoms is not a guarantee or even a sign of anything other than perhaps stress." She continued putting her earrings onto her ears, talking to him without eye contact, trying to keep her emotions intact. "He did a pelvic exam and didn't think I was. You have to wait for the fifth month for assurance because that is when you can hear the baby's heart sounds and when they start to move, and of course your body would have changed. There's also a strange urine test that involves frogs, but that's not necessary for me right now. Also, there's an X-ray you can do apparently at five months and you can see the whole bone structure, but that, again, is way down the line. A long way off . . ." Olivia's voice began to tremble.

"Hey, hey, don't get upset." Jonathan caressed her, but she pushed him away and stood up.

"I just don't understand. I have always been normal. There's nothing wrong with me. And yet nothing's happening."

"Of course there's nothing wrong with you, don't be silly. These things can take time—they don't always happen straight away."

"We don't have a lot of time!" Olivia said, no longer in control. "I've passed my midtwenties. I know women who have had three children by my age, and I can't even get pregnant with one!"

"Olivia, please, you're not too old. Don't be ridiculous."

"Ridiculous? How do you know? What do you know? You go off and travel and work and then come back and expect things to fit into place, and then when they don't you don't have any understanding as to why! Maybe getting pregnant isn't ever going to be something that can happen, Jonathan . . . then what are you going to do? What am I going to do?"

"I do know that stress and worry aren't going to help," Jonathan replied. "You need to calm down. I'm here now."

"You're here, and you're not." She tried to soften her tone.

"The war has torn families apart, destroyed people's lives from Napa to New York, and now it's supposed to be a time of healing, rebuilding, renewing our land and ourselves."

"You sound like a diplomat's wife."

"Jonathan, I'm trying to create a family for us, a life beyond the two of us, and all you do is focus on the Soviets and Washington's needs abroad. What about me? Your life with me? What about what is happening right here in front of you?"

Jonathan looked taken aback. "We moved here to keep you safe, to start our life, yes, but I don't care about making a life here forever. We need to be able to move and follow the needs of my job, you know that. I've been honest from the beginning, and you never seemed to mind before. In fact, I thought you enjoyed the idea."

"Except you don't bring me on any of your trips, your adventures. I'm supposed to stay here and make a home for you to return to. Make a family. You have dedicated your life to this country, first as an officer, and now as a diplomat. You're able to remain completely stoic and determined to make a difference from the inside out because . . . because . . . well, because your guilt is still there."

"What is that supposed to mean?"

"Leaving the war as a soldier before America ever started fighting in it. I see it, and I understand to some degree, but it doesn't leave a lot of space for me."

"That's not fair, Olivia."

"How the heck am I supposed to get pregnant when we only have intercourse once a month?"

The question came out like a slap. Their lovemaking was an issue that had never been discussed before, and Olivia nearly wanted to take it back. Nearly. Jonathan responded, as he always did, very matter-of-factly. "Olivia, I don't enjoy being away from you this much, if that's what you're asking, but my work is important. The country is depending on the Soviet negotiations going well, and yes, I have become a part of that. Frankly, that is more imperative right now than how quickly we conceive. We have time and you are just overreacting. I need to focus and prioritize whatever it is I'm being asked to do at work. And I need you to understand. I am not going to apologize for that."

"Apologize? You think that's what I'm after, an apology?"

"Well, what then?" She could hear the exasperation in his voice. "We'll keep trying for a baby, and sooner or later it'll happen."

"When?" Even as she said it, she knew there was no answer to this. Nevertheless, she looked at him in a defeated way, as if begging him to fix this. Fix her. "When do I get to start *my* life, Jonathan?" she implored.

"That's funny," he said quietly, "I thought you already had."

chapter four

1996

Cancer makes a house go quiet. It dominates every space, leaving its spill in every room. Vene wondered if the quiet was making it even worse for her mother, a woman who had always seemed to thrive on the flurry of activity around her. It was cancer, not her mother, that was now the center of attention, stage four bladder cancer to be precise, and there wasn't anything anyone could do about it. Time moved very slowly, and the only blessing was that her mother slept through most of it.

How had it come to this so quickly? Vene had deliberately stored her family tableau in a place where she could control it, never realizing the denial she was creating. Defeat by cancer was hard to reckon with, and they all dealt with it in their own ways. Her father spent much of the time reading in his study. But she was restless as ever. She checked her pager, the first time since arriving: one call from Dani, one from Tony, and that was it. She had told two friends and a few colleagues that she'd left for Napa to see her dying mother, and so far not one of them had thought to call and leave a message. Perhaps they didn't know what to say? How's your dying mother? Truth was, she didn't know herself.

Every time she thought about going into her mother's room, she paused, unsure of which way the conversation might go. She was loath to have another confrontation. Tony had said that now was the time to just love her and let go of grief; that is what he thought she was holding on to, grief about the relationship she'd never had with her and now never would.

She decided to stop in town before collecting Dani from the airport. She went into the kitchen to see if Max needed any shopping done, but he was nowhere to be found. She saw the cookbook, her mother's cookbook, on the counter and picked it up. She leafed through slowly from the beginning, stopping at every second or third page. There in the margins were notes, suggestions, thoughts that one might find in a diary of sorts, not a recipe book, and as she read them she became increasingly intrigued.

Hated this dish even though Max promised the time spent would be worth it. I've yet to see the point with this little fishy fish and feel like I'm missing something again.

Felt lonely today, and cold. This soup warmed every part of me, and it was a relief. Funny how soup warmed me more than an actual person could.

Jonathan's favorite starter at the moment—if only he knew.

If he only knew what? There were scribbles and notes on so many of the pages. Vene tried to picture her mother writing these words. Incredible how a mere recipe could lead to this outpouring of thoughts and emotions when the woman she knew always seemed devoid of analyzing deep feelings at all.

Hidden pleasures in the sauce—

made for a saucy night!

Saucy night? Pleasures in the sauce? Vene couldn't work out whether she sounded wanton or desperate, sharing a secret life with her food, for heaven's sake! She imagined her mother all by herself in this big kitchen, just as she was right then, with no one around for company except the ingredients to those recipes. Maybe that's why she started cooking, to avoid loneliness? There was clearly an ache in her mother that was expressed through her cooking. But then why had she stopped? Along with the emotional insights, she had drawn a symbol—a sort of circular vine-looking plant or flower surrounding a chalice. It appeared throughout the pages, each time more and more refined. Vene finally recognized it as the basis of the symbol they used on the back of their wine label. Was that how her mother came up with it, daydreaming in her cookbook? Vene traced it with her finger. Reading her mother's words felt like eavesdropping on a private conversation. But whom had her mother been talking to? Why would *lobster alla diavola* bring her to her knees? Devil lobster . . . her dad was allergic to shellfish, so had the indulgence of lobster been for herself? One thing she knew, there was passion on these pages, and in a bizarre sort of way, it made Vene want to cook.

She flipped through the book and found a recipe for chicken tetrazzini, named after the famous Italian opera star who had lived for many years in a San Francisco hotel. It looked easy enough to attempt, thanks to the annotations in the margin.

Easy enough to get right the first time!

6 lbs. stewing chicken

1 large sweet onion, chopped

2 teaspoons salt

4-ounce can roasted peppers

¼ teaspoon pepper

1 large green pepper, chopped

1 lb. spaghetti

1 lb. grated cheese

3 slices bacon, shredded

8-ounce can mushrooms

Okay, Mom, here goes, she decided. She could always say Max cooked it—he'd be mad but wouldn't tell. The recipe required time for the chicken to cook slowly in water in order to make a broth, so she had to get moving. Her mood instantly shifted. She was grateful for the focus, something to shape her day. Perhaps her mother had felt this too? She went into the pantry to check for ingredients. On the shelf between the spices was a small notebook hidden in plain sight. Vene hesitated before pulling it down. It was as if she was now in on her mother's secret, and clues were everywhere. Her mother had called the notebook "Dinnertime." Inside were recipes with star ratings next to them, along with funny lines like:

Ho ho hogwash—terrible idea for fish

Vomit vongole—forgot to make sure clams were fresh!!!

As well as more intimate ones . . .

Lost lasagne—I happily lost myself
today making this lasagne.

Gnocchi with butter sauce—surprising
how something so plain can taste so rewarding—
oh, how I wish for my life to be the same!

As she read through the pages, she pictured her mother in this exact pantry, sitting on a stool perhaps between the sage and cinnamon, writing down her observations and reflections. That spot had been a haven for Vene and her friends and their childhood secrets. Her mother must have done the same, only her imagination had been her companion. But surely cooking wasn't a hobby people just dropped. Why would someone work through so many recipes and then just stop, especially when it evoked so much emotion? How did this woman who knew each spice jar, who was so playful and passionate about food, become her mother? Cold. Unsentimental. Vene grabbed the cans of peppers and scoured the shelves for what she needed before heading out to town for the rest.

Oakville market was a short drive, and she'd been going there since she was a little girl. It was an old-fashioned market in the best sense of the word, supporting its community by selling only local produce and of course local wine. The Winstons had always supplied many cases of their family cab, and despite the high price, it always sold out. Vene pushed through the exit door to enter—a stupid joke she used to do as a kid that made her mother crazy—and there was nice old Mrs. Olsen still behind the counter.

"Hello, Mrs. Olsen," Vene said with a smile, taking a cart. She couldn't help but still call her Mrs. Olsen even though Vene was nearly fifty and Mrs. Olsen nearly eighty. Years ago, it had been Mrs. Olsen who had told her that her fake ID looked exactly that, fake, and that no one in San Francisco was going to believe that a seventeen-year-old was twenty-four. It might have been a good lesson had it not been for the fact that it had been Mrs. Olsen's own daughter, Hillary, who'd provided the ID in the first place.

The aisles smelled fragrant with fresh ingredients. As she wheeled her cart through, she saw a good friend of her mother's and sighed. That was the downside of a local market. There was no escaping seeing someone you knew, and regardless of whether you were in the mood or not, you had to stop. Mrs. Howard was the town gossip, and Vene slowed down grudgingly.

"Hello, Mrs. Howard, how are you?" she asked.

"Oh, Vene, dear, good to see you. Please, it's Barbara. How is your mother doing? I hear she's not well, but I didn't want to bother her."

"Ah, you're sweet to ask—not great, flu perhaps, but nothing to worry about." Damn, rumors flew faster than mosquitoes around there.

"Oh, honey, I'm so sorry. I only just saw her last month at a wine release reception, and she did look a bit tired. Please send her my best. I'll pop in during the week."

Vene wanted to tell her not to, that her visit might actually make her mother have a coronary on top of everything else, as she'd never want her friends to see her that way. But she knew that alerting Mrs. Howard to the dire circumstances of her mother's health would be like taking out an ad in the *Napa Valley Chronicle*, and that would be equally destructive.

"You know, Barbara, my mother wouldn't want anyone catching her nasty bug, so perhaps hold off on visiting till later." Any mention of germs always kept people at an arm's distance. "I'm just here buying food to cook for everyone so she can rest up."

"Well, that's a good thing. We all know just how much your mother hates cooking!" Barbara laughed. "'Thank God for Max!' was all she ever said to me. Well then, lovely to see you, Vene; it's been way too long. Hope you're here for longer than a few days this time. Please give my love to Dani and Robert."

"It's Tony," Vene replied stonily. "Dani and Tony. I remarried eight years ago."

"Yes, yes, of course," Barbara said with just enough of a tinge of knowingness that Vene could sense that her mother had shared her opinion of Tony more than once. Small towns—a reminder of why she'd left.

She gathered her ingredients and headed over to the check-out. To the side of the counter were books on the region and local wineries. Sure enough, there was the one from the Winston Family Estate, published because her mother had convinced her father it was a good marketing tool—*People love coffee table books*, she'd said. Vene hadn't yet seen it finished, which felt embarrassing at this moment, and took a minute to flick through all of the beautiful pictures, most in black-and-white, taken in the late '40s when her parents had first arrived. There were pictures of the vines, close-ups of the grapes, the lake, the cave, and outdoor shots of all the dwellings. Her father hadn't allowed any family photos except for one small one on the inside back cover—the three of them, down by the lake, smiling. It had been taken well after she'd left Robert, but Vene remembered how unwilling her mother had been to have Tony anywhere near the family portrait. The only other personal photo was a 1946 snap of her parents standing on either side of their award-winning winemaker, the Italian. They all looked so young. Her dad in his three-piece suit appeared ever so serious, and her mom, as always, looked incredibly stunning. They both stared stiffly at the camera without much expression while Vene noticed the winemaker's faint smile, as though acknowledging he was the odd one out.

"I love that book," Mrs. Olsen said, interrupting her thoughts. "People seem more interested in the heritage of Napa and the stories behind the labels these days. And the winemakers themselves are becoming like celebrities. Have you been to French Laundry yet for dinner? Apparently, you can't get a reservation."

"No, not yet. I hear it's amazing."

"The Europeans know their food and wine. Just like your famous winemaker, what was his name again? You know, the handsome Italian who brought over the French cabs and blended them?"

"Mr. Viandanti?" Vene said, looking at the photo. He was indeed very handsome.

"Yes, of course! Victor! We all remember Victor. He was quite something. Napa in the forties was so exciting." Vene was sure she detected a gleam in the woman's eye. Vene hadn't thought of Victor Viandanti in years, nor had she ever really known much about him.

"What happened to him? Is he still in Napa?" asked Mrs. Olsen, looking as though she'd like to look him up that very second.

"I have no idea," Vene replied, putting the book firmly back in its place. "I'm glad the book turned out so well. My mother was right after all."

Back at the house, all was still quiet. She dumped the bags on the kitchen counter just as Max entered. He might not have possessed the same energy of days gone by, but he was still in command of his domain. "Let me help you," he ordered, emptying the bags before she could say anything. "What have you got here?"

"I decided to make lunch for us all. I need to get started on the chicken before I go and collect Dani."

"That's not necessary. I am happy to do it," Max said.

"Max, I know you think my cooking is awful, but I looked at this recipe and I'm pretty sure I can do it. My mother made notes on this page too, so if my mother could do it, then I should be able to figure it out too, right?"

"Actually, she mastered a lot more than chicken tetrazzini," Max replied.

"Oh?"

"And using peppers she grew herself."

"Really?" she said, acknowledging Max's pointed comments.

"This is a summer dish," Max finished.

"I know, I mean, I know it's not summer, but the peppers are fresh from somewhere in the world, right? We have two cans to prove it!" Max didn't respond. "Honestly, Max, I just chose a dish that I thought I couldn't ruin."

"Cook," he relented. "It'll be good for you."

"What's that supposed to mean?" she asked, suddenly defensive.

"Listen, Vene. Much of who your mother was, is, is right here in this kitchen. So you should cook too; you'll feel closer to her, understand her better. Read the recipes. Read her notes, her thoughts . . . and cook." And with that, Max poured himself a glass of water and turned back to the sink, leaving Vene staring after him in surprise.

1946

Menu for Jonathan's family—meat, meat, meat

Fichi e prosciutto
Coniglio brasato
Funghi ripieni con salsiccia
Gelato al limone

Paired with
Beaulieu Vineyard, Georges de Latour,
Private Reserve Cabernet, 1945

Olivia spent hours contemplating the menu for Jonathan's parents' dinner. Each dish had been chosen specifically after a lot of trial and error. She knew that growing up they had eaten a great deal of rabbit and duck, whatever game had been shot that day, so she was confident they would be pleased with her choices. His parents had arrived the night before for a short visit to see all of the changes on the estate. Olivia had managed to excuse herself from drinks at the Mondavis' and a tour of the property to secretly attend to the preparations of the meal.

Something in her wanted to prove Jonathan wrong every time she stepped into the kitchen. This was about what she needed, even though he was ironically the beneficiary of hours of her experimenting. If she could be really good at something, provide for him in a way she was proud of, then maybe she wouldn't feel so empty all of the time. It had gone beyond just wanting his approval, and she was willing to do it behind his back if need be. Cooking made her feel alive in a life that often was full of numbness. All of which was probably why she found herself hiding in the pantry, waiting for Jonathan to go outside and finish the tour. She could hear him discussing with Max what time dinner should be served. She had told him she was at the dressmaker's, but here she was crouched down between the flour and sugar bins. She waited ten seconds after the outside door shut before carefully venturing out. Max gave her a slight nod that the coast was clear.

They continued where they left off. Max had shown her how to perfectly season the sausage meat for stuffing the mushrooms. Marjoram, thyme, bay leaf, oregano, basil, rosemary, and hot red peppers in many combinations. All these different herbs, especially in such generous quantities, wouldn't be used in American cooking, but in Italy they were part of everyday food. Max's mother, apparently, had gone overboard on the spices throughout his childhood, leaving his taste buds on the fiery side. What the Winston family was going to think about them was another matter altogether, and Olivia found a certain amount of mischievous amusement tossing in a few extra pinches of red pepper.

The truth was the Winstons could never imagine, understand, or accept that Olivia might derive a deep satisfaction from creating their dinner, aside from merely choosing the menu. But too hot, too salty, undercooked, overdone, not enough sauce—these were things she could fix, control, and master, unlike certain other aspects of her life. Cooking kept her dreaming. It kept her hopeful. Cooking allowed her to become increasingly in touch with the side of herself that yearned to be freer, wilder. Jonathan wanted her to embrace a formal role at the vineyard, but the only interest she had in the wine was how much to pour into her ragù.

"It's all yours, Max. Make sure the rabbit doesn't overcook. My in-laws like to see blood!" Olivia said with a snarl. She pushed the last of the sausage stuffing inside the mushrooms and wrote a few notes in the margin of the cookbook, something about wanting to murder someone, before washing her hands.

"Will do, Mrs. Winston. Blood dripping. Noted."

Olivia left Max and the kitchen staff to lay the table for dinner. Upstairs in her bedroom, she looked out the window and saw Jonathan standing amongst the vines with his father—both men in suits and ties as if they were going to the office. His mother, in her brown, stiff tweed skirt with matching jacket, was waiting on the side staring into the distance, seemingly concentrated on not ruining her shoes. She was still carrying her handbag over one arm, too untrusting to leave it inside unattended. Olivia had never seen her put it down except at mealtimes. She liked her mother-in-law, but the woman's formality stood in the way of actually getting to know her. She wasn't a warm person, and after trying for the first few years, Olivia decided her own mother was difficult enough to deal with without having to take on another.

She chose a pretty emerald dress, nothing too fancy, with a cinched waist and large front pleats that ran down to the hem beneath her knees. The dress's hidden pockets made it one of her favorites, somewhere to park her hands. She hummed lightly to herself and put on a bit of makeup. If she kept life simple, it mostly worked, she thought. She looked at herself in the mirror, examining her face, her eyes, her skin—porcelain and smooth. There was beauty and softness there. She didn't want to look for too long, though, never too long in case the eyes looking back at her reflected her emptiness.

Downstairs the smell of the food filled the hallways with aromatic delight. Jonathan and his parents were in the study having a drink by the time Olivia joined them.

"Darling, let me make you a drink. I think you'll like it. I had one in New York, and Mother has tried and loves it," Jonathan said with awkward enthusiasm. He was always trying to bridge the gap between his parents and his wife. He was wonderfully relaxed with his parents' formality, which reminded Olivia just how much he was like them.

But for her, every drink or meal with them felt forced. "What's in it?" she replied carefully.

"Vodka, ginger beer, and a slice of lime. We don't have lime, so I used lemon, but voilà . . . " Jonathan handed Olivia the drink in a special copper mug that kept it ice-cold. "It's called a Moscow Mule. John Martin, the East Coast spirits distributor I met with and the chap from the Cock 'n Bull who makes ginger beer, came up with it. They must have had a few, but by the time they figured out this combo, it really worked. It's got a great taste. A real zinger!"

Olivia took a sip. The spicy ginger with the vodka kick went down a treat. "Interesting. Delicious. Sweet even. I love the ginger."

"I love the vodka," joked Mrs. Winston. She seemed to have had a few already given how loudly her comment came out. Olivia looked to Jonathan, who quickly glanced at his father. It was a well-kept secret in the Winston family that the matriarch loved her cocktails, and everyone knew she was capable of saying just about anything when the vodka took hold . . . and it usually did.

"So, when are you two planning on starting a family? You know they say it's not healthy to wait too long," Mrs. Winston said with another gulp of her drink. "There are risks to the baby when you're older." And there it was. A truism not to be denied.

"Mother . . ." Jonathan said sharply. Mr. Winston discreetly placed his hand on his wife's arm.

"What?" she continued, ignoring them both. "Have you decided not to have children? That would be such a shame. Even unnatural. Olivia will be twenty-seven this year. People are inquiring."

"No woman likes their age discussed, Mother. Surely we can change the subject."

"No, you're right," Olivia finally said to Jonathan's mother. All eyes fell to Olivia. "I do like the vodka as much as the ginger. Now if you'll excuse me, I will go tell Max we are nearly ready for dinner."

Olivia escaped into the kitchen and sat on a stool. It was too easy to cry—his mother meant no real harm. She was the sort of woman who couldn't help pointing out whatever was missing from your life and highlighting it in red pen. It just made Olivia feel so very alone. Max walked in from the dining room. The prosciutto and figs had been placed for the first course, and the rest needed to come out of the oven. Olivia tossed the remains of her Moscow Mule down the sink and poured herself a splash of vino rosso from the open bottle on the counter.

"I can pour you something a little nicer than cooking wine," came a voice from behind her. She turned around to see a man holding a basket of grapes. She had no idea who he was, but from his gardening clothes, she guessed he was one of the new workers from the estate.

"I'm fine, thank you. Just changing the taste in my mouth," she replied, annoyed by his impertinence. "And you are?"

"Victor. Victor Viandanti," he said in a thick Italian accent, putting out his hand.

She stared at him imperiously for a moment, irritated at the intrusion, and then shook his hand. "Nice to meet you, Mr. Viandanti," she said frostily, wondering if his hand was clean.

But instead of letting go, Victor held onto her hand, forcing her eyes up to his. "Please, call me Victor."

To her utter surprise, she felt a current of something. Wonderful if rather odd, as though meeting someone important. She shook her head to dispel the thought while Victor merely smiled back at her with an easy comfort, only letting go of her hand when he felt her draw back. She suddenly felt vulnerable and very self-conscious.

Talking too quickly, she said, "Well, Victor, you can set the grapes down over there. We are quite busy right now getting dinner ready, so if you'll excuse me." Olivia motioned for him to leave the basket to the side and moved past him, carefully avoiding his eyes.

"It smells *veramente buono*, Max!" Victor said in his thick Italian accent as Max took the braised rabbit out of the oven. The sauce bubbled around the meat while the juices mixed with the rosemary, sage, and garlic in the dish.

"*Grazie*," Max replied with a quick look at Olivia, who couldn't help but feel proud. She lingered to see if more compliments were to follow. Max set the rabbit down and went back to the oven for the mushrooms.

"What wine will you be serving with it?" Victor asked Max.

"Beaulieu Vineyard, Georges de Latour, Private Reserve Cabernet, 1945," Max said, placing food onto trivets on the countertop. Olivia could hear Jonathan and her in-laws seating themselves in the dining room. She dipped her finger into the rabbit dish and tasted the flavors, exchanging a quick look of satisfaction with Max before she turned to leave the kitchen.

"*Lei fantastica*," Victor said admiringly to Max.

"Yes, she is," was all Max replied.

chapter five

1996

Napa Valley's local airport, Santa Rosa, was once an army airfield and originally used to train the US army fighter groups and squadrons during World War II. Jonathan had often traveled to and from this airfield during the war. Vene was always asking her dad for stories of his diplomatic travels. He was good at giving basic details of negotiations regarding trade policy and peace, but she never got much out of him that hadn't already been published elsewhere. She often felt their relationship itself was constrained by the Official Secrets Act. One day, she hoped, he'd talk to her about something personal.

She arrived early at the small terminal to collect Dani and sat down in the only area with scattered seating and some basic food choices. In front of her were a mom and her two small boys. The older one, probably no more than four, was trying to keep his army figurines out of the sticky hands of his little brother. Vene couldn't help but laugh, predicting it would end in tears. The mother was desperately trying to pretend the squabbling kids weren't hers just long enough to get a few sips in of her coffee, but it was not to be. Whammo—the two-year-old took a blow from his brother and began screaming, whereupon all eyes fell onto this exhausted mom as she was forced to grab them both back into her fold and scold them, her coffee spilling over all the while. Vene watched them with mixed feelings. She'd always wanted a sibling to play with, or beat up, and Lord knows she'd wanted one for Dani. When Dani was a toddler, she never slept; the excitement of the day woke her every morning before dawn. Vene finally surrendered to her daughter's spirit, failing the "healthy sleep patterns, healthy life" section of the parenting book, and found herself running, skipping, and playing endlessly with Dani at the craziest times of the day. She would fall into bed well before normal adult hours to preserve energy for the next early morning. Motherhood was endless.

On the left of Vene sat an elderly couple silently holding hands. They looked serene and sweet and unphased by the chaos around them. She wondered what their life looked like and how long they'd been wearing those matching wedding rings. Were they sweethearts from early days? First marriage? They certainly appeared content. She twirled her own ring around her finger. She and Tony had the three colors of gold intertwined as their wedding rings. Vene represented yellow gold, Tony white gold, and Dani was their rose. The interconnectedness appealed to her, as if they were more beautiful together than separate. Tony was the type of man who allowed her to be herself, no excuses, no apologies, and had always embraced Dani as his own. She had understood what made people want to get married when she met Tony. It wasn't just loyalty—it could also be love and desire. She moved gently through all these thoughts until there was an announcement on the loudspeaker and then headed eagerly to the arrival area.

At eighteen, Dani was well past her height at five foot nine and stunning looking—all legs, long wavy hair, big brown eyes like Vene's, and porcelain skin, but with girlish full cheeks that her mom envied. They both always felt lucky to be so close. Dani wanted her mom near and shared almost every thought in her head, which was both demanding and fulfilling. Their relationship was everything Vene's own experience as a daughter had not been . . . personal.

First off the plane, Dani spotted her and ran over, dropping her backpack and burying her head straight into her chest. They stood there for a long moment, Dani gripping her tightly. Vene was struck by how upset she was.

"Hi, Mom," Dani said eventually, wiping her tears and her face with her hands. "It's really good to see you. I can't believe it."

"Oh, honey." She gave her one more squeeze. Vene had been so wrapped up in her own misery she hadn't really contemplated how hard this would be for Dani. "Don't worry, your grandmother is still here, giving orders as usual. She'll be so happy to see you. Thank you for coming."

"Of course I'd come. I'd do anything for Grandma."

Really? Vene couldn't help thinking. How had her mother gained that position in Dani's life? The unconditional love element seemed so effortless between them. Yes, she was a very caring grandmother who was always there when asked, or needed. The joy her mother had felt when Dani came into this world had been enormous. She found everything Dani accomplished, however small, to be significant. Odd—annoying, even—considering she had never been one to show much emotion about most things Vene had ever done. Of course it wasn't a competition, but her mother's generous heart seemed to have skipped a generation, and Dani never noticed.

"Want something to drink for the ride?" Vene handed her some money.

"Sure." When has a teenager said no to money and a drink?

"Not Coke."

"Mom . . . I'm in college now. Guess what . . . they have a lot of Coke there, and I don't always drink it." Dani went into the shop with a toss of her hair.

The days were just starting to get colder. Vene found the car in the parking lot, put on the seat warmers, and pushed Dani's seat back as far as it would go, enjoying the feeling of being able to look after her girl again. She pulled the car around the front just in time to see Dani come out of the terminal, a Coke in hand.

1946

Rainy day fish menu for me and Max
(sarde lesson—oh my!)
Sarde al forno
Riso con gamberetti

An autumn vegetable garden in Napa smelled of fresh dirt and scattered herbs. Olivia picked the last of her parsley and carrots, cabbage and broccoli, feeling the sun setting on her back. She dug her fingers into the soil and scooped up the rewards of her planting. Doing this satisfied the part of her possessed by a desire to watch things grow. Some vegetables were bigger, some smaller, but most had survived under her watch.

Back inside preparing to cook, she kept looking out the window, something she found herself doing often these days. She was sure she'd seen a movement out of the corner of her eye. Yesterday, it was, in fact, a deer. Two actually, grazing on the corn. This time, she waited, but there was nothing—the darkness playing tricks on her. Once again, her thoughts drifted to that curious man, the one whose touch she remembered. *Victor Viandanti.* She said his name in her mind. And then once out loud. "Victor Viandanti." She liked the way it sounded, adding an Italian accent, emphasizing that he was from a land far away. When would he appear again and would it be as he had before, seemingly out of nowhere, marking that day as special with nothing more than a handshake? She was sure he'd held on longer than normal, staring right at her, daring her to look away first. And she had, of course; she had, but only after staring back.

How ridiculous, she scolded herself, to be wasting consideration on a man she didn't know, and what's more, worked for her! Nevertheless, since Jonathan had left on an extended work trip, she was aware of choosing more colorful dresses in the morning, taking more trouble with her hair, even reapplying lipstick several times a day. Aware too that once again she felt the excitement of being a woman. She gave herself a shake. It was silly; she ought to summon him to the house, if only to dispel the absurd notion that she wanted to hold his hand again.

Just then, Max entered the kitchen. "Good evening, Mrs. Winston. Is there anything I can assist with?"

Yes, Max, go find Mr. Viandanti and bring him to me at once, she wanted to say. "No, Max, I think I'm all set for our meal. I decided since Mr. Winston isn't home, we could sauté some of the shrimp you bought yesterday, and I could make a simple linguini pesto to go with it."

"Good choice. Did you already make the pesto? I'm not sure we have any pine nuts."

"Yes. Yes, we do, I mean, yes, I did," she said.

"And the wine?"

"What about the wine?"

"I think a white wine with a mineral taste would pair well with the shrimp. I could ask—"

Olivia interrupted, "You could ask?"

"I could ask one of the staff to go to the cellar and get a Gavi di Gavi from our Italian cases."

"Of course," she said, disappointed. "Sounds perfect. Perhaps, though, our new winemaker is around to ask . . . I mean, being Italian and all."

"Mr. Viandanti? No. I saw him drive up to his cottage a few minutes ago."

She was startled. So it could have been him in the window before? Oh Lord. Had he been looking back at her all that time? "Well then, thank you, Max. Please get someone to fetch a nice

chapter six

1996

It was early evening. The sun, huge and orange, slowly dipped into the cloud bank on the horizon. The top of it was still curved, but its lower half had collapsed as though resting after a long day. Two floor-to-ceiling windows looked out onto the vineyard from Olivia's room, a view that had saved many a depressing day. The door to the room was flung open.

"Dani, you should knock," Vene scolded from behind.

Her mother lay in bed reading, something she had begun to enjoy only recently. *Not enough time to read*, was what she always said, but now she read not to feel the time. Ignoring Vene, Dani threw herself on top of her beloved grandmother and wrapped herself around her frailty. She had always been free with her grandmother, and Olivia the same way back. It was the only time Vene fully saw the spirit of the love her mother had inside of her—unabashedly giving and receiving, nothing calculated or controlled. With Dani it was pure joy and Vene always felt resentful, a third wheel, not knowing how to join the group hug. As Dani cried, Olivia held on with more energy than Vene had seen since she'd arrived.

"Daniela," Olivia said softly, "oh my angel, Daniela . . . let me look at you."

Dani pulled away just enough for her to get a good look. "Grandma," she said with a huge smile, tears streaming down her face. As Vene watched them, she wondered whether Dani saw the blue veins protruding through thinned skin everywhere, how wrinkled and withdrawn her grandmother's face now looked. How her bones poked through her clothes like sharp edges. "How are you feeling? Are you in any pain?" she asked sweetly.

"I'm okay. Today was a good day. You look even more beautiful than before. And your hair, it's really lovely. I love this length on you."

"I cut some layers in. You really like it?"

"Love it. Gorgeous. Oh, I've missed you so much."

"Missed you too, Grandma." They hugged again.

"Your mother says you have a boyfriend."

"No, I don't," Dani said quickly, shooting her mother a weird look.

"No, I didn't," Vene reacted equally as fast.

"Well, a boy, anyway. Lord knows there will be loads."

"Oh, Grandma."

"Just promise me you will always follow your passion, your heart."

"I will, Grandma." She held her hand tenderly and sat beside her while Vene stayed at the foot of the bed like the family bottom feeder.

"Is that what you did, Mom? You followed your heart?" Vene chimed in.

Olivia looked at her with what appeared to be disdain. But disdain for what, Vene wondered.

"No, not always," Olivia replied with an audible sigh. "But then I had you, so responsibility took precedence."

"That sounds depressing. Having me sounds like a real burden."

"Burden, no. A change of direction, yes."

"You mean Mom wasn't planned, Grandma?" Dani added with a cheeky laugh, trying to lighten the mood.

"Planned . . . I had wanted a child for years. If you mean planned that way, then sure, she was planned. But what did I know about plans then? It was a time just after the war. Everyone made sacrifices. Everyone."

"I guess the moral of this story, Dani, is to make sure you don't get pregnant until you've fulfilled whatever it is that will make you happy before you get tied down to motherhood and lose your dreams." Vene couldn't help it; she felt furious and defensive, a familiar spiral of emotion.

"Ouch, Mom. That's a bit harsh."

"Just don't get pregnant. Until you really want a child." Vene looked at her mother, who took a sip of water and avoided Vene's eyes.

"I'm so not getting pregnant. Not for a very long time," Dani said.

"My generation made sacrifices too, Mom, but we're not war babies and so there is less guilt and dishonesty attached to them. The 'shove everything under the carpet' mentality. It's exhausting, don't you think?"

Dani looked at Vene incredulously, clearly not understanding the layers of conflict inside her mother's heart. Or her point.

"Sacrifices are choices too, and often made to better one's life," Vene added, trying to drive home some point she wasn't even sure of making.

"Hmph," Olivia said. "Sacrifices should be made for the greater good, for the family, not just for oneself. Women today don't realize how good they have it. The freedoms in life that are taken for granted. The problem with your generation is the narcissism, the self-interestedness that comes out of you—it abandons concepts like patience, morality, loyalty."

"Is that why you can't stand Tony? Because I wasn't loyal to a family portrait painted with a man I didn't really love? That I betrayed the 'Winston Family code of ethics' by not sticking with my man for better or way, way worse? What about being happy? Being human? Making mistakes—or I suppose you think you never made any unless it was in your Bolognese?"

"Mom . . ." Dani said, putting a restraining hand on her arm, but Vene brushed it away.

"My mistakes have shaped my life. Not sure what my sauce has to do with it," Olivia said, equally harshly. "As for Tony, he isn't for me to like. You made that perfectly clear."

"Really? Oh, really? You think your approval didn't matter? That it didn't keep me up night after night? That I had to make sure Tony was busy every time I wanted to come home and see you and Dad so he didn't realize how unwelcome he was? You made my life hell not accepting him, and that's why I decided to stay away. Is he just not good enough for you? Is that it? An Italian man who's too different from the old-school mold? Have you never just had to follow your heart, like you're telling Dani to?"

Olivia refused to rise. "Robert is a good man, and more to the point, he's Daniela's father. It is our responsibility to her to sustain that relationship," she shot back, her voice steely.

"Don't you dare tell me what is best for my daughter. Ever." Vene couldn't take any more fighting. It hadn't been her intention to confront her mother, in fact the opposite, but seeing her with Dani, she hadn't been able to stop herself. At that moment, her hatred tasted like old metal, potent and something she wanted to spit out. She and her mother only had two gears—one passive and the other very aggressive. Both were equally upsetting. Vene stormed out of the room and, just for childish good measure, slammed the door behind her.

1946

Olivia was alone in the kitchen. She and Max had decided to treat themselves as they had been out all day in the rain tending the garden. She felt inspired and had insisted on doing the cooking on her own, even though she knew from experience that sardines were an entire activity unto themselves and took time to prep. For a start, cleaning them was something of a delicate process. It involved descaling the skin, removing the head just above the gills, slicing the belly, and removing the intestines. It was important to make sure all of the guts were gone, as otherwise they left a very bitter taste. She ran her thumb along the backbone of each fish and butterflied it open, breaking its spine by the tail, using her forefinger and thumb and squeezing—before gently pulling it out completely. It was immensely satisfying how easily the backbone came out when done properly. Finally, she scraped off the sides of the fish with a knife, ridding it of any small rib bones and excess guts.

"Rumors Are Flying" by Frankie Carle was on the radio, and she found herself lost in the music. At that moment, the back door flung open and there was Victor, standing on the threshold. For a moment, she could only stare at him, aghast. All that thought and preparation put into when she would see him again and now here he was, standing right in front of her and more attractive than she remembered. She was acutely aware of her hair in disarray, her apron bloodied with fish guts, her unmade-up face.

He seemed to be waiting for something, and she took hold of herself with an effort. "Oh my goodness! You're soaking! Hurry, come inside," she said quickly, taking his arm and drawing him in, pushing the door shut against the howling wind and rain. Victor took off his coat and shook it near the door to keep the water in one area.

"I'm so sorry for the mess. It's really wild out there," Victor said, looking at the puddle of water on the floor.

Wordlessly, Olivia took his coat and put it on the back of a chair to dry. The radio was so loud it embarrassed her, and she quickly turned it down. She gave him a hand towel and tried not to watch as he dried his face and hands. He had a strong, interesting face, alive with curiosity, and a wonderful smile. He was flushed from the weather outside. Almost instinctively, she leaned back into the counter and found herself arching her back ever so slightly. He turned and caught her eye as he dried his hands.

"Ah, *sarde*," he said, picking up the little fish and smelling it. "The freshest fish smell like the sea they were living in. These are *molto buono*—very good."

"Yes," she managed, trying to gather her wits. Two minutes ago she had been completely in control of this space, and now it felt as though a tornado had swept through her kitchen. She resumed descaling the fish, busying herself to avoid looking at him. "Max got them today."

There followed what felt to her like an awkwardly long pause. Victor seemed quite happy just watching her, while she grew more uncomfortable and self-aware by the second. "Why are you still here?" she said, almost blaming him for something.

"Scusami?

"I mean now. Why are you still here so late? It's past six."

"Ah . . . I am working. Watching."

"Oh, I see," Olivia replied, not seeing at all. She attacked the little bones furiously.

"So, you are cooking again tonight?" Victor asked with a hint of knowingness.

"Yes, well, just this evening . . . usually Max does the cooking, but . . ."

"But you cook from the heart. A passion, no? You enjoy?"

Olivia looked up at him. How did he know this about her?

"My mother used to say," he continued, "'*una persona con il cuore di marmo non e stata nurita con l'amore.*'"

"Which means?"

"A person with a heart like marble has not been fed with love. You give love through your cooking. It makes those eating it . . . warm."

Olivia allowed herself a faint smile of soft enthusiasm. How easy it felt to be close to this stranger. And how loudly her heart beat every time he looked at her.

"May I help you?" Victor said simply.

Olivia's cheeks reddened. "Sure. I guess. If you like."

He came to stand next to her. He took a knife and a sardine, skillfully descaling and preparing the fish. She watched him closely. His hands were gentle yet firm, his arms strong. He had a way about him that implied he was completely in control. She had never felt such energy from a man before, and it seemed to flow through her own body. *Get a hold of yourself*, she thought sternly, trying to rein in her wandering mind. They worked for a few moments in silence, but for the faint music on the radio. Victor started to hum along to the song playing, never looking at her, completely at ease. Olivia was grateful for the distraction as she struggled to regain her composure. Just his presence at the sink, over the bones and filleted bodies of the fish, felt somehow intimate and somewhat inappropriate.

She continued descaling, and when she spoke next, it was casual, purposely matter-of-fact. "Jonathan tells me you're doing wonders with the vineyard." She felt the need to bring up her husband's name. "I didn't realize we hired a new winemaker. What happened to Paul, the old one?"

"Perhaps he was too old?" Victor said with a bit of humor, turning to her. "I think your husband wanted fresh ideas."

Olivia continued staring resolutely at the counter. "You've been in Napa for a few months, yes? Your English is very good."

"No, no, I came to America at the beginning of the war, when Italians could travel without too much problem. I have been in Napa for several years getting to know the land. As for my English, you are too kind." He inclined his head. "I still have much to learn even though I studied, if I'm honest, since I was a child."

"You've been here this whole time? It seems so strange that we've only just met. Shame . . ." This last word tumbled out of her mouth before she could prevent it, and when Victor didn't reply right away, it remained suspended in the air between them. "I mean, it would have been nice to infuse the vineyard with fresh ideas sooner," she added quickly, tugging down her apron as if a more pressed appearance might create a little authority.

"Well, I am here now, so . . ." he replied. Completely distracted, Olivia took another fish and mindlessly sliced open its belly. What was that supposed to mean? Was it innuendo, or was she imagining it? Victor was watching her, and she was caught between feeling self-conscious and intrigued. Suddenly, he put his hand over hers on the knife's handle. She held her breath. For Victor to touch her in her own kitchen? A member of the staff whom she barely knew? What would Max think if he walked in? But there was no way she was going to pull away. "It is better that you slice away from yourself, a cleaner cut like this," Victor instructed, taking another fish and slicing it expertly, his hand guiding hers. Olivia felt weak, her hand trembling underneath his. Who would have thought slicing fish open could be this sensual! Could he tell that she was shaking? Victor let go of her hand gently. "Forgive me," he said, "but it is easier to show you when we do it together."

"Yes, well." She wrenched her hand away. "You're quite the teacher."

"Certain things are technique and so once learned it is easy. Other things are all about feel, instinct. Adding something or another to a recipe is what makes each cook unique. You are different, is my guess."

"I will take that as a compliment. I don't know if I deserve it, but perhaps one day you can have a taste of something I make and decide for yourself."

"I would like that very much."

"Good." Finally, she brought herself to look at him, but coming up with anything further to say was beyond her.

"Well, I should be going," he said. "The rain has stopped. Until next time. *Buona notte*."

"Yes, good night."

Almost as abruptly as he arrived, he was gone, leaving Olivia struggling to make sense of what had just happened.

chapter seven

1996

There were certain family traditions that everyone relied upon for different reasons, and Jonathan Winston's birthday was one of them. It came before the holiday season, so the desire to be together and celebrate was still fresh. He enjoyed the attention and liked to throw a party for nearly every winemaker, wine producer, or retired politician in their region. Max would prep several weeks before the occasion, picking and choosing the menu that always included old favorites like lamb stew, potato gnocchi, and stuffed eggplant, along with the latest food fads like fried calamari, crab cakes, and cosmopolitans. Considering how modest her father was with most things in his life, the fact that he loved celebrating his birthday made Vene and everyone around him happy to do it. But this year, given her mother's poor health, no one was planning on any celebrations at all.

So for better or for worse, Vene decided to attempt a festive evening for him herself. After all, she had learned from the best. Her mother was the consummate hostess and knew just how to balance a perfect party. For Olivia, it was all in the details. A beautifully crafted menu, a signature cocktail, the dishes and lighting just so. Vene was far more random in her approach, banking on a wish and a prayer that things would turn out right. She had never really followed recipes and yet realized her mother could have been the author of an actual cookbook. Every time Vene stepped into the kitchen these days, she felt a little closer to her. As if reading her recipe books and finding her notes had somehow finally taken her inside her mother's head, even if her mother was none the wiser. Some people get recipes passed down to them like an inheritance; Vene's felt more like a treasure hunt.

She sat in the kitchen for a while looking around at the neat space. So much had changed on their property over the decades, but the kitchen had remained the same. Soft yellow-colored ovens circa 1950—no reason to replace a good appliance—stainless steel sink and adjoining countertops, Sub-Zero refrigerator, and freezers that had only been switched out once since they were first purchased in the '40s. And as ever, her mother's copy of *Il talismano della felicità* was resting in its lucite holder on the side. The kitchen was a reminder of things that remained constant in life, a comforting source of belonging. And for her mother, it was the place to create. *Il talismano della felicità*—the talisman of happiness. Happiness, now that was something they could all use right now.

She opened the book, and once again as the pressed purple flowers fell from inside the creased pages, her eyes were drawn to a symbol scrawled onto the top right corner. The pages were full of random stains and markings, folded-down corners with a sticky note or two, but remarkably the book was still intact. She touched the symbol and twirled the flowers with her fingers thoughtfully.

Meatballs!!

Failing to make these light and fluffy was bad timing tonight. Timing is something I never get right, and I have no idea how I'm going to change that. All I know is that I have to.

Recipe for Veal Chops

My heart yearns for the truth of who I am. If never a mother, then just a lover? Pair with the right wine and I shall be free.

Pair with the right wine and I shall be free . . . Hmm. What did she mean by that? Free from what? Vene wondered. The sentence had something earnest in it, desperate almost. She'd written it before getting pregnant, obviously. How much did not having a baby torment her? The words didn't seem upsetting, but she did sound trapped. And choosing a wine to set herself free? Perhaps it was nothing to do with a baby but a reference to a European trip where Jonathan had brought home wine. Could it have been a make-up dinner for being away so much? Her father might have opened a French Burgundy to apologize for his absence and it just so happened to go perfectly with the veal she prepared, so much so that the dinner was intimate and unexpectedly warm. Maybe her mother confessed to him that she had done the cooking that night. Always did the cooking for him. And it was her freedom from pretense, from her obligations as a stiff diplomat's wife that she finally felt released from. They could have got drunk together, a bit shy his first night back, but their guards going down as easily as the Burgundy. Vene read the line again. She had never given much thought to her parents as people—lovers, thinkers, and passionate beings in their own right. Does anyone? But it occurred to her then that the reality of their lives as a young couple in wartime must have been hard, separated and alone so often. Was this why they hadn't had more children?

It was true that her mother was emotionally distant and not very maternal, and that at times Vene thought her mother even behaved toward her as though she were allergic to her very existence, as if being reminded not to taste closeness. And after a while, Vene developed her own visceral reaction every time she noticed her mother's retreat. Or had it begun the other way around? Had their relationship somehow been *her* fault? Had she been a difficult child, grown into a bad daughter, and all along her mother had been reacting to her? For Vene's whole life, the coldness of their relationship filled her with such doubt and bewilderment. She had never managed to get beyond her mother's hard veneer. And yet the pages of this cookbook were alive with passion and intimacy. She had poured her heart into cooking long before she was a mother, but it seemed that once Vene was born her writings, her free spirit, her joy, ceased. It was a terrible indictment of her mother's feelings for her, and Vene felt cheated, confused, and utterly betrayed.

Spaghetti alle vongole

Food is more than sustenance—

food is passion, food is sensual.

Lamb stew

Don't use oregano, use fresh sage. Jonathan won't understand the difference, which is exactly what is wrong with him! The taste is in the details and patience is essential—my motto these days.

As Vene stared at the substitutions and the exclamation marks, her anger rose in her throat. All along it had been her mother, not Max, cooking her dad's birthday stew? She couldn't get her head around it—why had her mother kept it a secret, why had she never cooked for her own daughter, taught, showed her any of this, brought her into her life this way? Cooking surely could have been an easy bridge for them.

Mutinously, she turned more pages. *Fine!* Vene would cook the main dish, the beloved lamb stew. She'd follow her mother's instructions and make it for the family. It was clearly a risk given the fact that she'd never made stew before, but too bad. How hard could it be? Her mother reserved all her patience and concern for food? She literally seemed more vulnerable with her spaghetti vongole than with Vene!

As she prepared the lamb, cut off the fat and cubed the meat, chopped the onions, pancetta, and gathered the herbs, she soon stopped feeling nervous and angry. There was a rhythm to cooking that cleared the mind. Cooking was comfortable and predictably linear. Do this to the meat, and then that will happen. First, she seared the lamb in batches, adding a few herbs in the pan as instructed to infuse the oil. She took a long inhale of the aroma she'd created—not bad. She turned on the radio and found an oldies station. "Ten Cents a Dance" was being sung by Anita O'Day, who re-recorded the hit in 1930, and soon she was humming and jiving along to the music. More searing and chopping, combining vegetables with the meat, adding dashes of salt, pepper, garlic powder. Confident now, she grabbed a few random spices not in the recipe and threw them in as well. Pleased with herself, she tasted the stew. Holy crap—it was way, way too spicy. *What the . . . ?* She double-checked the label on the spice jar. Shit—cayenne pepper! She'd put cayenne pepper all over the stew! Oh God, the meat sizzled away, rapidly absorbing the spice, and she didn't know what to add to calm it down. Quickly, she read the recipe again. Perhaps more tomatoes, or would that make it too saucy? Stock—did stock evaporate enough? Did they even have any more? How much stock was too much stock? She hated cooking, the pressure!

She had an idea. She opened the freezer, and sure enough there was some Tupperware labelled "stew" inside. She ran boiling water over it and dumped the entire thing into her cast-iron dish, watching the frozen lumps slowly dissolve. She had no idea if the stew meant lamb, chicken, or venison, but after she tasted her version again, she realized it didn't matter. There wasn't enough time to start from scratch, so it was either this or Domino's for the birthday meal. But to admit defeat to her mother wasn't an option.

1946

Menu for an easy dinner—
comfort food and chocolate

Zuppa di pomodoro
Salsiccia e patate
Torta al cioccolato

It was an unusually warm evening. Olivia had spent much of the day perfecting cannelloni and making pizza dough, which she then traded with her neighbor, Mrs. Taylor, for some much-needed beets for Max's soup. She wasn't a huge fan of beets, but Max insisted she would change her mind after tasting his mother's recipe. With Jonathan away she had the time and space to experiment in the kitchen and began living a life totally separate from the one she led when he was home. It felt odd at first, spending more and more hours with Max in the kitchen and garden, but these last few days in particular she hadn't been able to wait for her next cooking lesson. It was an awakening of sorts, and along with her newfound freedom, she was aware of a yearning for a man whose face entered her mind far too often. The more she cooked, the more she found herself escaping into a fantasy about when she would see Victor next. And even as she battled such forbidden thoughts, more and more came.

It was late in the afternoon by the time she excused herself from Max for a walk before sunset. She had heard Max mention that Victor was back at his cottage, and there would be no harm in walking in that direction on the off chance he was around. A random encounter, she would say if she saw him. The cottage was tucked away at the top of the property, separated from all other buildings; nevertheless, it was almost opposite to one of her favorite spots on the estate—a hill with a beautiful view of the valley below. And no sooner had she reached it than she heard his shout.

"Hello!"

She hesitated, a strange and wonderful sensation filling her. She waved, wondering whether she should leave it at that or whether she dare go across and see him. It was one thing to plan an encounter, quite another to actually go through with it. Victor motioned for her to come down. She knew she looked radiant, in a mustard-yellow dress cinched at the waist with pleats down to her mid-calf, topped off with a cardigan sweater. It was hardly the typical walking outfit, but then taking a walk hadn't been her primary purpose.

He was sitting at a table on the porch in front of his cottage. It was the kind of porch that could have had a rocking chair but didn't. On the table three different bottles of red wine were laid out in front of him. They were all from past vintages, all single-grape cabernet varietals for a comparative taste test.

"Drinking on the job?" she joked awkwardly as she walked down to the porch.

"Drinking for the job," he replied, smiling back at her. "Join me."

She took one last look around to see if she could be spotted, hesitated, then sat down next to him facing the rolling hills and dipping sun. He had papers all over the table, research notes on soil changes and the different weather patterns from year to year. He poured her a taste of each of the three wines. "Tell me what you think."

She relaxed a little, swirling the glass of the first before taking a sip. "That's a lovely wine. Not too much of any one flavor, really. Very easy."

"Okay. Yes. But first, before you drink, you must smell." He took the second glass and swirled the wine around in it, tilting it sideways to see the color and the "legs"—a winemaker's term for the streaks that trickled down the side. Then he stuck his entire nose into the glass and inhaled deeply. He handed it to her. "Try."

She took the glass and mimicked his moves, swirling and smelling the wine. "All this for a taste."

"All this for the right taste. Wine is complex and rich in texture. You need to determine all the different notes you taste; the aroma tells a story about the earth, fresh soil, and decaying leaves, whether the grapes were picked too early or too late. Here at the estate, we plant on the hillside where the soil is rockier and a smaller crop thrives best, producing smaller grapes of higher concentrated color and flavors." He poured the third wine. "Now try this." He handed her the glass, and once again she swirled and sniffed. "I want to use different storage for this year's vintage," he said, "oak barrels like the French, and see how it works moving forward."

"Do they do that here in Napa?" she asked, trying to follow along, noting that he intended to stay for a while.

"There's a man here named André Tchelistcheff. He came at the beginning of the war to work for Georges de Latour. He's considered one of the best winemakers at the Pasteur Institute in France, and he is the one who brought the modern winemaking techniques from Europe, using the French oak barrels for aging the wine as well as proper sanitation. This third wine is from his technique of storing wine."

"It's very good," she said, not really knowing what to say.

"I like André very much, and he's doing here what I was doing in Italy. Planting vineyards with higher levels of density, reducing the amount of sulfur, and using high-quality French grape varietals. I also use my Italian root stalks."

"Is he the one responsible for the success at Beaulieu Vineyard?"

"Exactly."

"Yes, I have heard of him." Olivia had heard of all of these winemakers but never cared much about the process. Until now. Now she wished she had paid more attention. "Winemakers are like artists, I'm told."

"Artists, perhaps. But artists in need of a canvas." Victor looked out onto the estate. "Together we will make exquisite world-class wine here. You'll see."

Olivia blushed. Victor was looking at her in a way Jonathan never did. He said the word "together" as if their futures were interlinked. She had never thought of planning with a man before; it was always planning by a man or for a man. He picked up the third glass again and moved it under his nose, and then to hers. She smiled shakily and inhaled.

"I smell the fruit, but it's not fruity, it's . . . well, there's a deeper smell, a bit fuller . . ."

"And?"

"And," she continued, wanting to get it right, "wait, let me taste again." She took another sip. "It's somehow jammy? And I can taste the tannins around my mouth . . ."

"And on your tongue?"

"Yes, and on my tongue . . ." She felt another schoolgirl blush rising.

Victor didn't take his eyes off of her. She was aware only of wanting him to touch her. And then, very slowly, as if commanded by her desire, he raised his hand to her face and with one finger wiped the lingering wine off her lips. Instead of flinching away, she found herself leaning in toward him, and still he stared at her as the light changed and moved around them. Time seemed to stop, allowing for a moment full of hope, magic and forbidden. She felt his lips slowly press against hers and linger for a moment, and then he pulled away.

"Forgive me," he said simply.

"For what?"

"Perhaps it's the wine," he said unconvincingly.

“It must be,” she agreed.

“You are very beautiful, Olivia.”

She dragged her eyes from his. The last of the sunlight dipped, and darkness began its descent. It was easier to be in his presence without light, and there was a part of her that could have stayed there all night long. “I should be going,” she said, “before it’s too late.” The double meaning was not lost on either of them. She knew if she stayed any longer, she would give herself away completely, if she hadn’t already. She got up quickly.

“I’ll walk you,” Victor said.

“No, no, I know my way so well, and Max will be looking for me.” She couldn’t risk anyone seeing her with him at night. What would they think? What did she think? “I need to finish cooking . . .” She spoke hesitantly, unsure of herself. “Thank you for the wine, and the lesson, and . . . well . . . goodbye!” She quickly turned and started up the hill. At the top she stopped, unable to resist checking whether he was looking after her. When she turned back, she was aware of the cheekiest grin covering her face.

chapter eight

1996

It was late in the afternoon. Exhausted, Vene collapsed into her father's big leather armchair. Dinner had taken so much effort—it just wasn't worth it in the end. The truth was, she hated cooking. When Dani was born, she'd had the desire to be that mom—the one who cooked everything herself from scratch, God forbid buying the quick meals in the jars, only to destroy the simplest of recipes. When she was married to Robert, he had been sternly judgmental. Over and over again, she had failed his happy homemaker's test. So after a while, she gave up. Tony could eat boiled chicken and be satisfied, so there had been no need to expand her repertoire, nor did she have any desire. With her own work hours, she did a lot of eating on the go, so her cooking just got rustier and rustier. The one thing, though, that she had absorbed from watching Max all those years was that if there was enough love in the food (along with the freshest of ingredients and an entire bottle of Winston cabernet in the sauce!), it might end up being all right.

She heard music coming from the kitchen. Time to check the stew again. Max stood over the pot, stirring it around.

"Did you taste it?" she asked apprehensively.

"Yes."

"Oh." She stood next to him and looked forlornly down at the dark mess. "Does it need anything?"

Max didn't answer.

"I guess I should taste it?" Max just cleared his throat. She took a spoon and dipped it in. Well, it wasn't *inedible*, she thought. It just wasn't good. The Bee Gees came on the radio and started to belt out "How Deep Is Your Love." *To hell with it*, Vene thought. She grabbed Max's hand, ignoring his bemused look. She twirled around. "Come on, Max, dance with me—it's not like the stew can get worse."

"You'd be surprised," Max said nervously, eyeing the dirty pots and pans strewn all over the counter.

"Oh, come on, Max. I'm all stressed out from cooking. It's more fun to dance! There's not much left to tidy."

"I can see that," he said wryly as he looked around. Max had an enormous soft spot for Vene, and she knew it. He caved and let her take his other hand. She was sure he hadn't danced in ages, but he still had all the moves. He led her around the kitchen island, avoiding the handles of the pots and pans. She could see the huge mess around the countertops grabbing his attention as they dipped to the left and right, but she didn't let him stop. Max had always been an excellent dancer. Though he moved his feet as little as possible, he still somehow managed to maneuver her on beat, and she whirled from his side back to the counter, until Barry Gibb finished on one final silky note and they stopped, breathless and grinning.

"You still got it, Max!" she exclaimed.

She turned at the sound of clapping. Her father stood in the passageway applauding the performance.

"Bravo. That's my girl," he said.

"It was all Max," Vene replied, beaming. Max immediately busied himself behind the counter, looking embarrassed.

"I came in to say we will be one more for dinner tonight, Max. My wife will unfortunately remain upstairs, but my old associate Jenny will be joining us. She wouldn't miss your birthday stew."

Max and Vene exchanged a look.

"What?" Jonathan said, looking from one to the other. "Is something wrong?"

"Er, I'm cooking it this year, Dad."

"You?" Her father stared at her incredulously. "But darling, you can't cook."

"Don't worry, I followed the recipe and the notes precisely. Well, nearly . . ."

He looked troubled. "But this is Max's signature dish. He always makes it on my birthday."

"Well, actually, Dad . . ."

"Don't worry, sir," Max interrupted, "I'm sure Vene will do it just as well. And I'll be here, just in case."

"Yes, well, the Mondavis will arrive at seven o'clock, I'm told, just before the others, so let's have hors d'oeuvres in my study, shall we?" He didn't look that pleased.

"I got this, Dad. Really. Just have a good day, and let me, and Max, take care of it all for you."

"Why you've suddenly found the urge to cook is beyond me," her father said, sounding bewildered.

"Well, I've cooked it with love, so we'll see what happens. Seems like most of your favorite recipes were followed that way."

She could see he didn't understand, but maybe it didn't matter.

1946

Menu—an exploration of fall vegetables
Great use of what's ready to harvest
(My favorite eggplant dish by far)

Verdure stagionali
Pomodori ripieni di riso
Piselli con prosciutto
Parmigiana di melanzane

For most people living in Napa, harvest time was about the grapes. For Olivia, it was about her vegetables. The fall brought great riches: artichokes, green beans, beets, broccoli, and cabbage, along with carrots, chard, corn, peppers, peas, and parsley. She had been inspired during the war years to plant as a part of the war effort. The government had put a ration on foods like sugar, butter, milk, cheese, eggs, coffee, meat, and canned goods. Labor and transportation shortages made it hard to harvest and move fruits and vegetables to market, so people began planting their own "victory gardens" to provide these items for themselves and their communities, all in the name of patriotism. Olivia's garden was spectacular.

The early morning sun shone against the dew on the grass. The plants glistened with spiderwebs. Olivia bent over her artichokes, pulling out unwanted stalks to make room for new shoots. Some had already opened, their glorious deep-purple flowers reaching out to the sky. It seemed a shame to pick something so beautiful. She felt a touch on her shoulder and jumped.

Victor was smiling down at her. "Good morning. Sorry. I didn't mean to scare you."

"Oh! Hello . . ." she faltered, thankful for her big straw hat hiding her reddening cheeks. "I wasn't expecting to see anyone this morning."

"I can go," he said.

"No, please . . . stay. I never have company when I'm gardening." She waved the shears in her hand at the view. "It's so magnificent here."

"Yes," he said, still looking at her and not at the scenery. "*Bellissima*."

Blushing even more furiously, Olivia continued with her shears and cut a few artichokes, making sure to leave on each an inch or two of stem, but thinking all the while how much she'd like to kiss him, knowing it was madness.

"These are all ripe?" Victor said.

"The way you know is the shape. You want them to look like a cone with the leaves not yet open but big enough to show it's fully grown." Olivia pointed out a perfect artichoke. "Like this one, see? You can tell the heart will still be tender because its leaves protect it. This one over here, it's too relaxed, open just enough to make the meat tough. There's only one main artichoke per stalk, then usually two offshoots where another smaller one will grow. I love these purple ones." She realized she was talking too much but continued. "The globe ones are rounder and much bigger, but I like these ones."

"They are called Violetto artichokes," Victor said. "They are an Italian heirloom." He smiled, and Olivia realized he knew a great deal more about artichokes and probably everything else than she did. She could never speak to Jonathan about such things as trivial as artichokes, and yet here was a man as interested as she was. "In Italy, we grow everything." Victor kneeled down beside her and helped collect the artichokes from the ground and place them in her basket. "These are wonderful." He made a bouquet from some purple needle-nose flowering weeds, smelled it, and then handed it to her. "Out of the cultivated ground comes the wild plant, perhaps unwanted at first, but with its own beauty and unexpected value."

Olivia took the flowers from him and inhaled their fruity scent. She no longer felt shy. They were nestled down into the plants, so she leaned into him. He kissed her. *What am I doing?* she thought dreamily. Insanity.

"Come," Victor said, "I want to show you something." He reached for her hand.

They walked through the gardens and toward the vines. The morning song of the birds had given way to chirping and chatter. There was no one around, so she enjoyed his warm hand in hers. Strong and protective. It was a relief to not have to speak. So many thoughts were racing through her mind. She had only ever slept with one man, her husband. There had been a few flirtations before she met Jonathan, but she'd never pursued any of them. Jonathan was ten years older than her, and now here was Victor, another older man. She wasn't intimidated by his age; she was attracted to it. Both men possessed authority and wisdom, which she found alluring, yet Victor still seemed to have a desire to learn—learn from her, learn with her. Her experience with men might have been limited, but she knew she was feeling something exceptional. She was sure of that.

He led her around the back of the estate toward the vineyard. Four acres of vines that flowed onto rolling hills. The harvest was over, but most of the vines still had scattered red and golden leaves left on them. Wildflowers were growing in between, bright yellow buds exploding up through the soil, life still blooming before the winter frost. At the top end of one of the rows, Olivia noticed that all the wooden planks attached to the vines had been painted green. Victor stopped.

"These plants, this vine, they came from Italy," he said.

"How do you mean?"

"I brought cuttings with me when I came to America and grafted them to plants here in Napa several years ago. When I came to your estate, I replanted them here."

"Why?"

"Why?" he repeated.

"Why did you come to America?"

"Yes, of course." Victor laughed, and then fell silent, as if not knowing where to begin with his life story. "It had been a relief for me to be in a country where no one knew my name," he said, "my family name, my history. The sense of freedom at the end of the war was new for everyone, and the wounds were raw for most. My hatred for Mussolini and fascism was not just mine. Nearly every corner of my motherland had been touched or destroyed by it."

For a moment, he looked disturbed. "When I left Italy," he continued quietly, "I left in a hurry just before we joined forces with Germany. I was a winemaker among other things, and my family owned land. We had a responsibility of culture and tradition to uphold—banking, trade, politics, agriculture. For hundreds of years, my family prospered and dominated, *eravamo aristocratici importanti.* And we had influence over how we lived, how we worked with farmers and other traders. Our workers were part of our family, and their happiness wasn't separate from mine. For years, Il Duce's slow and steady grip on my country and its people haunted me. But it didn't change our ways. Until it did."

"What do you mean?"

"My father, he had to adhere to the new laws being imposed on landowners; we were being watched—how much money was given to the government, what we were paying the workers. They lost all their rights. And I was the eldest son. I had to uphold this fascist agenda without a voice. I felt very angry and isolated in my own home, and I could no longer accept Mussolini's tyranny. I was close to my workers and believed in their co-ownership of some of the land they worked their whole lives, some for generations, to obtain. I wanted to give them what was rightfully theirs. But to do that would have put my family at risk. You simply were not allowed to disagree with the new regulations. And these regulations contravened everything I believed in, everything I was. So I had to leave."

"Go on," Olivia said quietly.

"There was a man, Louis Martini, an Italian who came back to Italy to taste the new wine I was blending. I was doing something different, innovative—a new technique of blending, discovering a new taste in Italian wine. I used the beauty in other grapes outside of our region, outside of Italy, and appreciated their value. It was rare to look toward France or America for anything, even just a few months ago. But why not blend a sangiovese grape with a French Bordeaux or even a Napa cabernet grape? This experiment was not popular, but I didn't care. No one listened, though . . . until Louis came to visit."

"I've met Louis. He and Robert Mondavi have dined here many times. I had no idea that was how Jonathan found you."

"Louis, he made it possible for me to come to California. To Napa. He had done his own experimenting just after Prohibition with planting pinot noir and chardonnay in Carneros when people thought it crazy, and also a lot of cabernet grapes here and in Sonoma. My leaving was more of an escape, and because of that I have tried to stay . . . how do you say in English, among the shadows?"

Olivia remembered friends talking about the fear and paranoia of Italian immigrants who lived in the coastal California towns during the war. Even now people were wary, despite Napa remaining full of European settlers. "But how long are you going to stay? Will you ever go back?"

"For me, it was always worth leaving if I could take my beliefs with me. I believe in self-expression. I believe in free thought. And I believe in wine," he said with a smile.

Olivia laughed.

"You laugh, but wine is about understanding where you are, what soil is under your feet literally, how to create something of value from basic methods of growth and blending of elements. It's a life lesson, not just a wine lesson. Sometimes we all have to ask ourselves, *Who do I want to be?*" He looked closely at her. "Who are you, Olivia? What are you made of?"

These were questions she had never asked herself. "I don't know," she answered honestly.

Victor touched the vines. "It is hard to know these answers when all you do and all that you are is for the benefit of other people. I hear my father in my head every time I want to speak about Italy. But his decisions and connection to Italy are different from mine; his voice in my head isn't my voice. You must find your own voice. Wine was the only thing I knew that was pure, and so I built my life around it."

There was so much to take in. She had never asked herself what she really wanted before. She touched her fingertips to the vines. That these plants right here were the fruits of one man's determination to hold on to his sense of self—this seemed fantastic to her, so unlikely, and yet here they were.

"A winemaker is only as good as the wine he produces," Victor said. "I wanted to make my mark here, at the Winston Estate. Here was a perfect place without a real winemaker in charge, and it was the best opportunity to do my work. Wine in the Napa region is changing, and I have no doubt the world will soon realize this. That was my first reason. But now I have a second reason."

He looked at her unflinchingly, and Olivia found her heart was pounding so hard she could hear it in her ears. The land, the valley, had never meant much to her until that moment. She had always wanted to dream with Jonathan, but his relationship with the vineyard and estate was strictly business, emotionless. But there in that moment, the very soil underneath her fingernails felt precious. She felt connected to nature and all the myriad treasures it provided, and the feeling was intoxicating.

"Thank you for that," she said quietly.

chapter nine

1996

The table was laid for her father's birthday meal. It was the first time in months the dining room had been used at all. Most meals were served either in the kitchen or upstairs in the master bedroom where a makeshift table had been set up. It was at her mother's insistence that the family eat in the dining room that birthday night, especially since Dani was still there and guests were attending. It seemed at the end of one's life, tradition was the one constant everyone could rely upon. Even from a cordoned-off bedroom upstairs, her mother still held the capacity to control the night, and in this case, Vene admired that.

The house smelled of sweet meat. Whether it was a good or bad smell, Vene honestly couldn't say. Besides, there were so many little details to remember: light the candles in the guest bathroom, make sure the trolley bar was fully stocked in her father's study, gather wood for the fire, check all the glasses and table cards. Max knew the routine, but Vene hadn't been the hostess of a formal dinner in ages, let alone one at the estate. It felt odd knowing her mother was unable to come down, and yet selfishly it was a chance for her to be with her father without any second-guessing or judgment. Her relationship with her dad was uncomplicated, probably the healthiest bond she had. She knew he could use some extra care that day of all days, but why, oh why had she chosen to cook his special meal as a way of expressing her love for him? She hadn't really thought it through, and now there was no going back. What if it was genuinely awful?

The doorbell rang. Oh God . . . she could picture her mother's face enjoying the unfolding spectacle even from upstairs. The first guest arrival always came too early, and invariably it was the Mondavis. She could hear her father ushering them into his study for drinks. The Taylors would almost certainly be next. Sure enough, before she could rip her apron off, the doorbell rang again. This time Max received them. Should she taste the stew? She was almost too scared to try it. The doorbell sounded a third time. It had to be Jenny, her father's retired secretary. Seeing her would make Vene relax, so she abandoned the stew to answer the door herself.

"Hello, Jenny! It's so nice to see you," she said. Jenny exuded ease and warmth. She had always made an effort to connect with Vene during her childhood, which Vene appreciated. She instantly felt less nervous.

"Vene. Look at you. You're so beautiful," Jenny said with a huge smile as they hugged. "It's been too long."

Ever the generous woman, she was holding a small box and some flowers. It must have been at least a year since Vene had seen her last, and Vene's memory of Jenny held fewer lines in her face and less caution in her movement. Her hair was completely white and bobbed, gently tucked behind each ear, and she wore her signature wool skirt to her knees along with a silk blouse and a sweater tied over her shoulders, a '50s fashion plate frozen in time. She also wore her signature pearl necklace—a sign of her generation for sure—and her wedding ring from her late husband. Vene had wondered at the time of his death, twenty years earlier, whether she'd ever remove the ring, and the answer clearly was no. A solemn promise symbolized in gold meant a lot to some. Jenny was the same age as her mother, a stark reminder that her mother's life was being cut short all too soon.

"Dad's having birthday drinks in his study, Jenny. The usual suspects are here . . . well, a few, anyway. And Dani was able to stay."

"Oh, good," Jenny said. "Here, I brought these for your mother. How is she?" she asked, handing a bunch of flowers to Vene. "Will she be coming down?"

How little people knew, even close family friends. "No, she's going to . . . Well, she's just not able to join us."

"Oh, what a shame."

"Yes, but she wants us to have a lovely dinner—and for Dad, we will." Vene smiled, taking her arm and leading her into the study. There was a comfort being with Jenny. Her constancy, her loyalty to her father. It had been that way as long as Vene could remember. Jenny would sort out this and that; she was always there when the family needed anything. She remembered being so mad at her mom when she was little that she insisted Jenny move in and be her mommy instead. That hadn't gone down too well. But Jenny was always devoted, with no apparent agenda, or certainly none that Vene ever noticed. She was glad she and her father had remained so friendly even after his retirement.

In the study, Robert Mondavi was telling a story about how he and Francis Ford Coppola met. Apparently, Coppola had been shunned by the community back in the '70s, and no one showed up to his housewarming party apart from the Mondavis. It was then that Robert told Coppola about Napa wine and its heritage and his beliefs on how to be both a successful wine producer and accepted by the community. Many gave him credit for Coppola's restoration of the Inglenook brand as a premium winery. Jonathan looked affectionately across the room as Jenny entered. "Ah, Jenny, so good of you to come," he said, embracing her.

"Of course, always," she replied, handing him the small box. "Open it," she said eagerly.

He looked at her. "Now?" he asked, eyeing the others, and she nodded. He opened it. Inside was a vintage pocket watch made of sterling silver, with a crystal face in perfect condition, the movement signed by Frodsham and Baker. "How on earth did you find this?" he exclaimed, inspecting the watch with awe.

"I've been looking for some time," she replied proudly. "Apparently, this was Frodsham's cousin, Edward, who continued in the watchmaking business. This one was made in 1885 . . . as opposed to the others we saw from the later period."

"Oh, Jenny, clever, clever. Thank you ever so much," he said.

The details of the gift were clearly a part of an ongoing conversation, and her father was looking at Jenny with so much tenderness that Vene suddenly felt awkward watching.

Max entered. "Dinner is served," he announced. Vene looked at Max to get an inkling as to just *how* the food turned out, but he was giving nothing away. Dani helped escort all the guests into the dining room, so Vene went into the kitchen for her day of reckoning with the stew. She reread the recipe one more time to make sure she hadn't missed a step. Her eyes traveled to the comments written in the margins.

Don't use oregano, use fresh sage. J won't understand the difference, but he'll taste it . . . just like all the other flavors of the meal. He seems to have his own palate these days, and nothing includes me.

Annoyingly, her mother's tips were never about the actual cooking. What was she talking about, his own palate? The other flavors of this birthday meal, the other flavors of what? And then it struck her—or at least, the possibility of it struck her. Jenny. Jenny was always at every single birthday meal. But why? She was only his secretary, and yet on any important or meaningful occasion, there she was. Could she have been another "flavor" of the meal? Was she the one "changing his palate"? The more Vene thought about it, the more it made sense. Jenny was the opposite of her mother, soft and warmhearted. She would have filled her father's life in a completely different way. For Vene, seeing her father through an adult lens was something she had never consciously done before. She kept him as a placeholder in her heart, father/hero, someone who loved and lived in a way she understood and accepted. He gave her mother security, strength, and unconditional love, but now it occurred to her . . . in return for what? Often for nothing, it seemed. Theirs was an old-fashioned, formal relationship, but she'd never questioned his choices up until now.

She tried to imagine Jenny with her father. It was a betrayal of her mother, but strangely she didn't feel angry or particularly upset. Was that awful? But how could she blame him? The only tenderness she'd ever seen in her mother was when she held Dani—never with anyone or anything else. It had always felt as though her heart was shrouded, rolled in yards of fabric, protected from any feeling. But what if she was wrong? Vene thought. What if she'd gotten everything the wrong way around? What if her mother had been the tender one, but her heart had been broken by her father's affair? What if the shroud was a blanket? She felt almost sure there had been some betrayal between her parents—the question was, whose?

1946

Menu for a night to remember!

"Lobster and the devil"

Zuppa di fagioli Toscana

Aragosta alla diavola

Zabaglione

It had been over a month since Jonathan went away on business. Olivia noticed that Max had never bought so much shellfish for their dishes. With Jonathan's potent allergies, he never dared have it near the counters, let alone cooking in the oven. But Jonathan wasn't home, and her passion for food and for cooking seemed to have unleashed something inside of her that Max clearly enjoyed watching.

It had also become quite normal for Victor to join them for dinner. At first, the usual formalities kept Max, Olivia, and Victor as separate entities in the same space. Max continued to run the household, Victor was the winemaker developing the Winston brand, and Olivia's influence over the gardens and interiors was soon refocused to cooking as her culinary fascination grew. She loved being in the kitchen experimenting with ingredients, spices, meats, and herbs with *a forza vitale*, as Victor would say—a life force. Rosemary, basil, marjoram, bay leaf, red pepper. The list was endless, but it was an authentic taste she was after. She played around with traditional Italian recipes, writing notes all over her book, before and after meals—marinating, tasting, baking, frying, sautéing vegetables, meats, and fish. With Jonathan gone, she felt free, and her cooking kept getting better and better. And it would have simply been a waste, Max said, to have no one to share the culinary delights with—so dinners were laid for three.

Early one evening, Max came back from town with three enormous lobsters. Olivia's eyes lit up. It was rare to be able to buy lobsters these days.

"Oh Lord, Max, those are incredible! *Aragosta alla diavola*—devil lobster. We're going to bake them in all their glory." She picked one up and inspected its claws. "I'll ask Victor to pick out a beautiful bottle to match these creatures." It had already come to feel quite natural to share her excitement with Victor. She raced out to look for him in the vineyard, finding him down by the lake at the entrance to the estate's cave, a passageway Olivia had yet to ever really explore. Dug by shovel and pick in the late 1800s, the huge cave on the Winston estate was notorious for its intricate pathways but hadn't been utilized for storage in years. There were so many stories about how the laborers originally built these caves—work that was done after finishing the construction of the tunnels over the Sierra Nevada Mountains for the Union Pacific Transcontinental Railroad. They were known to work daylight through candlelight, removing the excavated material in wicker baskets to get the job done. There weren't many vineyards in Napa with these kinds of caves, so inheriting one was a considerable privilege. Part of Victor's expertise was his knowledge of how to utilize the space that naturally provided high humidity and cool temperatures, ideal for storing and aging wine. The high humidity minimized evaporation, and the consistency of temperature at an average of 58 degrees was optimal for storage. Victor was just making a few notes when Olivia approached.

"Ah, there you are," she said breathlessly, "I had a feeling you'd be here."

"Yes, I'm here," Victor replied with a smile.

"Yes, of course." There was a discomfited moment between them. "I just wanted to say that Max got us a real treat for dinner, and I thought you'd want to pick the perfect wine to go with it." Her voice echoed loudly in the quiet of the cave. "Lobster, no less."

"You pick it." He took her hand and, before she could refuse, led her deeper into the cave. It was chilly and the light was dim. Victor lit a few of the lanterns perched on the walls. He took off his jacket and placed it around Olivia's shoulders.

"Thank you," she said. She felt a surge in her body, a rush of excitement as she followed him deeper into the dimming light. She stayed close behind, listening as he talked about the caves and their history, here and in Italy. But all she could think of was how she wanted to touch him, hold him, brush her face against his soft stubble.

"Here they are—I knew I put these bottles down somewhere." He stopped at a barrel and picked up a bottle. "I had some of these sent from Italy once I arrived. It has . . . *profumo splendido* . . . an incredible bouquet," he explained, turning to her, "like you."

He stood there, looking down at her. Olivia felt weak with desire. She leaned against the stone wall for support, the world around her shutting down—all thought of wrongdoing gone. He put the bottle down on the ground, stepped close and traced his finger against her lips, then her cheek, outlining the shape of her face. She closed her eyes and let her head rest against the wall. She could smell his scent, pine needles and sage mingled with salty sweat. She sighed as he slowly circled his fingers on the outside of her sweater, then around her erect nipples.

"Ahhh," she breathed involuntarily.

He slipped his hands behind her, pressing her body to his. She wrapped her arms around him, wanting more, needing more, feeling him rising firm in his cotton pants. They kissed and her body melted. They moved to the ground, clumsily, shakily, driven by lust. She ran her hands under his clothes. The muscles in his chest, his arms, felt strong and powerful. He lifted her sweater and kissed her breasts. She pulled him closer, craving all of him.

She felt wanton—free, able to feel everything, think of nothing. He pushed into her forcefully, and she gasped. For so long her body had felt broken, but now as they moved together slowly, lost in their own time, it felt fluid, perfect and whole.

chapter ten

1996

Olivia was reading in her bed. Jonathan had given her his latest crime novel by James Patterson, and she actually seemed to be enjoying it. All those years spent watching him read Grisham and Rankin, Connelly and Ellroy, King and Crichton, seemingly mindless literature of no interest to her, and yet now it filled her quiet days with pleasure. Vene was standing inside her mother's dressing room next door, sifting through the normally locked closet of her gowns—each perfectly preserved, stuffed with paper, and wrapped in thick, see-through plastic.

Next to her lay three dresses—a Coco Chanel, a Christian Dior, and a Balenciaga—draped over a chair like beautiful ladies-in-waiting at a ball. They were all from the 1950s, the golden age of couture, the moment when the frugality of postwar fashion finally returned to glamour and opulence. These were beautiful, but not the one Vene was searching for. She pulled out two more before finally finding it: the Hubert de Givenchy strapless evening dress. It was a stunner—cream lace over silk, with a bustier-style top, a tiny waist from which fabric flowed to the floor in gentle pleats, finishing in a small train at the back.

"Here you are," Vene said, as if greeting a long-lost friend.

"Did you find it?" her mother called out.

"Yes, yes I did," Vene replied, hooking the hanger on the outside of the door.

"Well, put it on then," Olivia urged.

Vene took off her clothes, unzipped the dress, and stepped into it. That gown was the most beautiful piece of clothing she had ever seen, or dared to wear. She tied her hair into a bun.

"You were so thin!" she shouted out as she sucked in her stomach as much as she could, attempting to zip up the dress from the back.

"Come and let me see," Olivia replied. She sat up in bed and took off her reading glasses.

Vene walked into the bedroom and stopped in front of her bed. Her mother looked at her proudly.

"You look really beautiful."

Vene twirled around a few times, enjoying the feeling of her mother's approval and in awe of her that she'd been able to pull off such a grand design.

"It's magnificent." Vene admired herself in the long wooden full-length mirror. "I look like you."

Her mother saw it too. Vene watched her taking in the sight and wondered if she remembered the role reversal, how Vene used to stare at her mother in the mirror whenever she was getting ready for her fancy events. How even as a little girl, Vene had marveled at her mother's beauty, hoping she would look just like her when she grew up. But Olivia's expression wasn't easily distinguishable. Perhaps she held onto other memories of these dresses than Vene did, those of a time Vene was only just discovering. Nevertheless, Vene pressed on.

"Tell me again about the night you wore it," Vene prompted.

"Ah," Olivia sighed, but now with a smile, knowing the storybook memory her daughter held dear. Vene had heard the story many, many, times but never got tired of it. "Audrey Hepburn had made a young Givenchy famous amongst the social elite. We were in London, 1953. You were just six. Your father and I were having a formal dinner party, and he had bought me this dress. He was no longer the ambassador, but we did still entertain Europe's most interesting politicians—including that night the deputy prime minister, Anthony Eden. I was already downstairs greeting our guests when you made your own entrance. You were wearing your ballerina costume, the one with the enormous sequined tutu. And my red lipstick. You walked slowly down the spiral staircase holding on to the banister with one hand, and your other arm outstretched very gracefully. Well, all the guests oohed and aahed and thought you were the most elegant princess. Later that night, at the end of the evening, I found you asleep on the top step of the staircase, still in your tutu. You used to love listening to the dinner parties below, all the adults talking and laughing. The sounds lulled you to sleep, I think. I scooped you up into my arms, and you woke up long enough to tell me not to take off your tutu—that you were a princess just like Mommy."

They were so rare, these moments, Vene thought, when her mother told her childhood stories, when they connected and bonded through a shared memory. What happened? How had it gone so wrong? Surely that memory was a happy one. Once again, Vene was overcome with doubt. Was it her? Had she been responsible for changing something so simple into the complicated relationship it was today?

"Did you ever get to wear the dress again?"

"No, I don't think I ever did," Olivia replied. "Most of those gowns have only been worn once or twice. It's a shame. I wanted to keep them, perhaps wear them again, yet in the end they just stayed put away." She paused, perhaps realizing how sad that sounded.

"I have so many memories of you dressed up in them," Vene said, "it would be nice not to lock them all away again."

"Of course," her mother agreed. "You're right. They should go to a worthwhile home," she continued, her eyes dropping away. "Maybe Dani would like to have a few?"

Vene added timidly, "Or me. At least one."

"Oh. Sure—take whatever you want."

"Thank you, Mom. I'll be careful with them."

1946

Menu—starring truffles!
I've never experienced something so explosive
yet subtle all in one, delizioso.
Tortino di tartufo
Risotto alla parmigiana con tartufo
Biscotti al cioccolato
Paired with
Brunello 1944, Castiglion del Bosco

Olivia felt alive for the first time in her life. Jonathan was away endlessly on business. She had no diplomatic wifely duties and thus had a huge space in her life, which was now filled with desire. Victor was all she thought about. Victor, and cooking. She was lost in a world of sensuality, her body, her heart, her every sense. Cooking had become the creative outlet where she experimented obsessively, relishing the result, good or bad. She was as wild in her cooking as she was with her emotions—pushing herself further, daring to take risks.

The house felt alive too. The air filled with energy, wonderful smells, a feeling of lightness. Olivia spent hours cooking stews and different kinds of meats, making pasta from scratch, and baking biscotti dipped in chocolate and serving them with fresh ice cream. There was no part of the meal she didn't attempt, and the kitchen was a mess of flour and spices covering every countertop. Max had temporarily given over his domain and had resigned himself to mopping up her mess as she experimented with venison, rabbit, and duck; gnocchi, tagliatelle, and lasagna.

One evening during dinner prep, Victor joined her. She and Victor always took great care not to be too informal with one another when Max was around. They had no idea what Max knew or didn't, but it was never discussed and neither of them wanted to put him in a difficult position. Victor placed a jar of what looked like rice on top of the counter.

"What is this?" Olivia said suspiciously.

"Open it," Victor replied. "But keep your eyes closed."

Intrigued, Olivia looked to Max and then to Victor. She closed her eyes and opened the lid. Victor took it from her and held it to her nose. She smelled the starch of the rice with a hint of something else. He spooned something out of the rice that was embedded inside and again held it up.

"Now smell again," he instructed.

Victor had taught her how to rely on her sense of smell when it came to cooking. She inhaled dirt, trees, and fungus. With her eyes still shut, she touched it under the crumbles of soil. It was something she had never cooked with before.

"Truffles," Olivia said.

European "tartufo" had never been successfully harvested in Napa, and Olivia had only experienced this delicacy on a trip to France before the war. There she had enjoyed the black truffles, but never the white ones that almost solely came from the small town of Alba in Northern Italy. Foraged by special pigs, they had a unique smell—newly plowed soil, fall rain, and burrowing earthworms—and their taste was equally complex.

"*Tartufi bianchi d'Alba*," Victor said, "from near my home. I had a friend bring me some recently. I can't believe they weren't confiscated; I know many who have been very unlucky, especially given the cost. But here they are."

"Wonderful!" Olivia exclaimed.

"Let the cooking begin," Victor said.

White truffles perfume the food they are shaved upon. It's unusual to use them for every dish in a meal, but Victor was insistent. Olivia used an old Italian recipe for thinly sliced boiled potatoes with truffle and parmigiana on top, along with a risotto decorated with yet more of the exquisite shavings. Victor had also brought a classic sangiovese Italian brunello from his personal collection—earthy and bold yet still fruity and round. He decanted it slowly in anticipation of the great feast. Max was left in charge of making the chocolate biscotti, and it wasn't until the fourth ring of the telephone in the hallway that anyone realized someone was calling.

"Good evening," Max answered, "Winston residence, may I help you?" There was a pause, and then he said, "Yes, sir. Mrs. Winston is in the kitchen, sir, shall I get her?" Hearing Max say "sir" broke the spell Olivia was under. Without looking at Victor, she quickly went into the hallway.

"Hello, Jonathan. It must be so early over there. Is everything all right? . . . Yes, yes, I even heard about the Paris conference on the radio news program. It all sounds promising, no? . . . Oh, well, that's good. I . . . I thought—no, no, go on . . . I'm sure it's difficult . . . the Soviets were always going to be tricky . . . Are you still returning next week? . . . Oh, I see."

She understood fully, more than most in fact, how in this postwar climate all diplomatic channels from the US were being used to help negotiate with Allied powers their positions regarding monetary reparations, territorial adjustments. Jonathan was in Paris having just flown over Normandy to help in the Paris Peace Conference. Out the plane's window, he said, he'd seen the devastation from the war and all that had been destroyed during the landings. It was getting harder and harder to separate the characters in front of him from the disaster on the ground. It was exhausting work, and the Soviet's demands were uncompromising. He tried explaining how their idea of presenting acceptable treaties for public approval was almost laughable—"Soviet public opinion" was an oxymoron at best.

Olivia looked down at her hand. Her mind wandered. She had taken off her wedding ring a few weeks ago when she was bathing and never put it back on. She wriggled her fingers around, turning her hand upside down and then back again. The lack of a ring made her feel free, and she liked it. She heard him mention his time frame. "Does Jenny have all of your information? Oh . . . she's with you? . . . Oh, I see, yes, well, good to have your team. I'm sure you're all exhausted. And emotional . . . I said *emotional*, you know, from the weight of the importance of it all . . . No, forget it, it's not what I meant, just forget it. Okay, well, I can only hope for all of our sakes that it works to our country's advantage."

There was a long pause and Olivia felt uncomfortable. She had wanted to say something important or profound, given all that he was confiding, and felt foolish at the attempt. The silence between them was always awkward, and the physical miles made it more so. "Jonathan?" Olivia tried to figure out what she actually wanted to say, but even as she began to talk, Jonathan was already apologizing for cutting her short. "I understand," she said, "you don't have time for long conversations, and it must cost a fortune, this call, so I will let you go. I'll call Jenny if I need you."

Olivia hung up and stood in the hallway. She'd known their lives would change after the war, but she honestly hadn't thought she'd be where she was right now—Jonathan solving the world's problems and losing his wife in the process. And yet all she could think of in that moment was that her heart ached not for the person she had lost, but for the one she had found.

chapter eleven

1996

Dani was baking in the kitchen. Ever since she was a kid, she'd loved to bake. "Not cook," she would say, "bake." If it didn't involve sugar, she wasn't interested. Max had taught her a thing or two about tiramisu and panna cotta, but chocolate flourless cake was her favorite. Before leaving, she was determined to bake it for her grandmother.

The kitchen was a mess. She was an untidy cook, and her ingredients were always strewn all over the floor as well as the counter, the sink, her hair. She didn't care, let alone notice. She liked to wear one of Max's aprons, the one that said, *I don't need a recipe, I'm Italian*. Max sat at the end of the counter waiting to pounce as soon as she let him clean up. Dani put the cake in the oven and set the timer.

"Mom, when the timer goes off, can you take the cake out? I need to shower and get ready to leave."

"Aren't I taking you?"

"No, Josh is," she explained with a slight smile. The "non-boyfriend" had clearly been promoted. Vene tried not responding.

"What? Why are you looking at me like that?" Dani said.

"I'm not looking at you like anything. I just thought I was taking you."

"It's no big deal. He offered and I said okay. It is okay, right?"

"Of course it is."

"I don't know, he's good-looking. And nice, but I'm not sure," Dani said, answering the unasked question.

"Well, the good news is you don't have to be. Trust me . . . you'll know when you know."

"I hope you're right. It'd be nice if it happened before I got really old."

Max laughed at this.

"It's true, Max," she insisted, turning to him. "Most of my friends have been in love at least once or twice by now. I'm seriously behind."

"What would her grandmother say to that, I wonder?" Vene said, smiling at Max.

"You're still very young," Max said.

"Precisely. Dani, I love you, but you sound ridiculous. When you fall in love, you won't have control over any of it anyway, so you may as well enjoy this part while it lasts."

"Jesus, Mom, you make it sound so scary."

This time Vene had to laugh. "Ha! Scary, no. Well, sometimes it's scary. Falling in love can be totally overwhelming."

Dani gave her a hug. "Love you, Mama."

"Love you too, pumpkin."

Dani gave Max a hug from behind and looked around the kitchen at the chaos. "At least it smells good, right, Max?"

Max took her apron from her. "*Ha un odore delizioso*," he said, smiling.

"Thank you, Max. Okay, I'm going to go get ready. I hate leaving . . ."

It was always funny to Vene to hear how often Dani told her she hated leaving the estate. At Dani's age, Vene had felt caged here. But to her daughter, it remained the land of dreams, a place to feel free. Vene poured herself some more coffee and waited for the timer.

"She's going to fall hard when she falls," she told Max. "Oh boy, we are in for a ride with Dani, I fear." Max nodded his head in amusement. "Did I ever tell you the full story of how Tony and I met? I mean, when we first met?"

"I'm guessing I need refreshing," Max replied, without stopping his work.

Vene took this as a sign that he was at least interested in the story she rarely got to tell. "Robert was away on business again, and Dani and I were living out our normal routine of school runs, playdates, homework, ballet lessons. I was in the supermarket lost in thought, and pushed my cart up to the cashier. I was about a third of the way into unloading my stuff when the man behind me touched my shoulder and said, 'Excuse me, but unless you're going to pay for my food, maybe you should give me back my cart?' I didn't know what he was talking about until I looked down and realized that aside from the lamb chops and yogurts, none of the other items looked familiar. Especially the Old Spice. I was so embarrassed. I had taken this poor guy's cart from an aisle and pushed it all the way to the cashier without noticing. We both laughed pretty hard. He was cute, I thought, and I liked his T-shirt. It was tight on his chest without being too tight, and I noticed how fit he was. Oh, sorry," she said, lifting her coffee cup so Max could clean underneath.

"Anyway, it was a funny, odd moment. I thought of him that night, but that was that. But the following week, I was in a local coffee bar, reading a book, waiting for Dani's ballet lesson to finish when I got this weird feeling, and something made me look up. There in line ordering coffee was the guy from the supermarket. If I hadn't looked up, who knows if he would have seen me. I watched him order. He was wearing an old pair of Levi's and another very sexy T-shirt. I wanted to go over and say hello but felt too shy. Instead, I pretended to be leaving and started gathering my stuff. It worked. He looked over and spotted me."

Vene remembered how it felt seeing Tony that day. "It was so weird, Max, there was a knowingness in the way he looked at me—as if to say, 'I see you.' He came over and introduced himself. Oh my God, my heart was pounding. I desperately tried to pretend it wasn't and at the same time thought, *Why the hell is my heart pounding?!* We talked so long that I was late picking up Dani. We spoke about art, and I told him I liked this local painter who lived in Venice, and he had actually bought one of her paintings the year before. He gave me his number and invited me over to see it. And so I did . . . I think I knew I shouldn't have, but I couldn't stop thinking about him and told myself that if I saw him again, I could at least stop fantasizing about him." She stopped, waiting to see if Max showed any disapproval. But Max was a keeper of secrets in the house of Winston because he wasn't judgmental.

She checked the timer. "We carried on seeing each other. I knew it was wrong, but I didn't feel guilty at all. And then I got pregnant. It was a game changer. I knew it was his. My first feeling was total elation that my real life was about to start. Not that Dani wasn't part of that, but Robert never touched my heart in the same way Tony did. Ever." She paused. "And then we came home for Dani's summer vacation. I told my mother, thinking that she would help me figure out how to leave Robert and marry Tony and have this glorious baby. We'd never really spoken about deep emotions that much before, but I wanted her support—I needed her help. But I should have known better. She told me I was going to ruin my life. That I had to protect Dani . . . I was so confused, I didn't know who to turn to. I convinced myself I had no choice."

The timer went off. Max opened the oven to check the cake. The smell of chocolate filled the air. She wondered what he was thinking. What would he have advised her had she asked him instead at the time? "I had the abortion," she said heavily. "Two days later, I left Robert."

Max nodded. He clearly didn't know what to say, and she didn't know why she'd suddenly blurted out the story. Nevertheless, it felt good, so she continued.

"Never to have a child with the man I truly love has been a curse. I thought I'd get over it, but I haven't. My mother made me feel so guilty. But she couldn't possibly understand the love I felt for Tony and that doing the right thing meant having the baby. And I was stupid enough to listen, and got rid of the thing I wanted most in the world. And now look at the dirty little trick life played on me in return. Life telling me I'd had my chance and blown it—refusing to give me another."

Years of anger filled her eyes. She knew that acceptance—of her mother, of herself, of all of it—was the only way through that pain. "I know what you're thinking, Max. I should just let it the hell go—that it's not my mother's fault. That there's no way she could have understood that kind of love, the agony of that choice."

"Decisions were made, Vene, with the best of intentions. I don't think blaming yourself, or your mother, is going to make your life any better. Or make any more sense. So yes, I'd say it's time to let it go." And with that, he turned to take the cake out and let it settle.

1946

Olivia and Victor lay naked in bed under the thick, soft covers. Her head rested on his chest, and he stroked her back absentmindedly. The glass windows of Victor's cottage glowed amber from the flames of the woodburning stove.

"I can hear your heart beating," she said.

"That's a good thing," he joked.

"It's calming. Beat, beat, beat . . ."

"It's quite fast, no?"

"Yes. Are you excited or something?"

He smiled. Then he took her chin in his hands and tilted her face up to his. "How could I not be?" He leaned down and kissed her slowly. They lay silently in each other's arms, Olivia's head once more against his heart.

"Have you ever been to Rome?" she asked.

"Of course. Many times. I have family who live there."

"How far is it from Tuscany?"

"By train, just a few hours."

"I always dreamed of going there when I was younger. My father loved watching films at the theater on a Saturday afternoon. Long before the war. He would smoke his pipe, and I would eat candy. I remember seeing *The Sign of the Cross*, set in ancient Rome. It was about this soldier torn between his love for a woman and his loyalty to Emperor Nero. I pictured myself as Elissa Landi, the Italian actress who fell in love with Fredric March—oooh, he was so handsome."

"This is why you want to see Roma?"

"No . . . well, yes, but, well, every time I think of Rome, I think of romance."

"Then I shall show you Rome."

"I'd like that," Olivia said simply. Never had she felt as happy or as at ease as when she was in his arms. This illicit romance made her feel strong, dare to dream. She inhaled his smell deeply. She could lie with him for hours, she thought, perhaps even forever.

chapter twelve

1996

Getting Olivia into her wheelchair took at least two people. One to carry the weight of her body, as most of her muscles no longer helped in the process, and the other to make sure that sitting in the chair was as painless as possible and that her clothing and legs looked appropriate. These days she was skin and bones. For a woman who had always needed to present herself a certain way to the world, minimizing her pain now took precedence. Max still insisted on doing the heavy lifting, which was borderline stupid given his age, but this time it was Vene, instead of the housekeeper or nurse, who helped position the pillows behind her mother's back and her legs on the footrest. Her mother needed help for the most basic of things, and Vene could see it made her vulnerable. Having her mother rely on her and show her weakness were two notions far, far removed from the reality of their relationship, and they both felt it. Vene's doula training should have counted for something, but it didn't. She fumbled through even the most basic of nursing needs, acutely aware of her mother's eyes on her. Fate had a mysterious way of working, and perhaps it was no accident that in this last stage of her mother's life, this uneasy closeness was being forced upon both of them.

It was another unusually warm day, and Vene had suggested a walk. Her father had the paths around the gardens mowed so that the wheelchair could pass alongside most of the flower beds and through some vines surrounding the house. She placed a wool blanket across her mother's legs, quickly tucking in the sides with precision, so as not to seem too fussy. Her mother untucked it almost immediately. Vene held up elegant slippers her dad had bought to make her mother feel more dressed up, as if she was going somewhere. Her mother nodded her approval, and Vene slipped them onto her feet and then placed them on the metal pedals of the chair. Max began to push her toward the elevator. Growing up, Vene had always found it odd having an elevator in their three-story house. But for homes built in the late 1800s, having an elevator was a sign of prestige. Nonetheless, it had rarely been used until now.

Downstairs, Max opened the back door to the garden where a ramp had been installed. The air was crisp and smelled of freshly cut grass. Vene breathed in deeply. Her mother closed her eyes and did the same.

"It's nice out here," Vene said.

"Yes. It was a good idea to walk," Olivia replied.

"Thank you, Max, I think I've got it from here," Vene said.

"Max should come," Olivia said to neither of them in particular.

"It's okay, Mom, I don't need help pushing you. Besides, Max is in the middle of cooking lunch, and could use a break himself. Max, you should get some fresh air later—it's good for you as well."

"Thank you, I might just do that," Max said, looking happy to give them some time on their own.

Vene started pushing the wheelchair up the garden's narrowly paved path. The chair was heavier than she'd expected, but she pretended not to notice. It was coming to the end of fall now, and the colors were changing. Bright greens mixed with oranges and blazing reds, sunshine yellows behind brown, shriveling leaves. And as always, the purple needle-nose poked its head through the dying weeds surrounding it. Olivia leaned over to collect a few.

"I like those too," Vene commented. "Funny how it's the random weeds that grab our attention."

"There's nothing random about these," her mother replied with a curt tone.

Vene's heart sank at how agitated she already sounded. "Well, they are weeds, and sure, they're indigenous, but most people would try having them removed. I'm just saying that I find them really pretty as well."

"Anything is worth admiring if it makes you feel something, Vene. I learned that from this place a long time ago."

Vene continued to push the chair, feeling the usual anger rising. Now the weight felt even heavier, and she tensed through each turn. She tried to ignore a sense of loneliness whenever her mother shut her down like that, seemingly out of nowhere, and so she focused on the task of going for a walk. After all, her mother was the one in the wheelchair; she was the one who must be frustrated. Vene pushed on, in and around the flower beds, up toward the top of the hill where some of the vines were planted. She consciously took another deep breath. "This entire garden makes me feel something," Vene said evenly. "I nearly stayed and worked here because of how much I love it. My life would have been so different. It's weird to think about that sometimes. It was a very special place to grow up. I know that now. In fact, there's a lot I know now, Mom, a lot we could share." Her thoughts were racing around her mind like a spinning top, each color representing a different one. This was a moment—pick the subject and go for it.

Olivia replied, "It takes intuition to run an estate. Not just the business, but also the land, the grapes, all of it. Your father always said you would have been great at it."

"Well, that's nice of him to say, but I'm not sure it's true."

"It's true."

"Thanks." *Was that a compliment?*

They watched the view for a moment. "As for loving this place," Olivia said, "I discovered love here, and believe me, it lasts a lifetime."

"It kept you married all this time."

"Yes, it did."

"Better to die having loved than never at all. Even when it's messy." Vene waited for her mother to respond, but she didn't. "Is that why you guys came back? After London?" She probed, "I mean . . . because your relationship did better back here?"

"Not really."

"You and Dad started your life here. Found love. You built something together here."

"Let's go to the top of the hill."

Vene started to push the wheelchair up the rickety crossing onto the hill toward the Italian grapevines. Almost all the other vines had lost most of their leaves except the more robust sangiovese grapes, whose colors were still in their full fall glory. She spun the chair around so her mother could see the view down onto the valley. She thought of all the things she wanted to say to her . . . all the things she wanted her to know. "This view never gets old. I can see why you stayed all these years."

"And I can see why you left."

"Really?" Vene asked. "Do you really understand why I had to leave? Because I honestly want you to understand that it wasn't Tony's fault. He would have lived anywhere. It was me . . ." She paused. If she threw out a bomb, there would be consequences. But it was time to be brave. "It was me, and it was you." She didn't dare look at her mother.

"Me? That's ridiculous. And unnecessary."

Now Vene stared at her mother. "What does that even mean? I'm really trying, wanting, to just be honest with you. I'm not looking to blame anyone, but time is not exactly on our side anymore, Mom, and I want you—I need you—to understand why I stay away."

Olivia looked past her at the horizon.

"I never meant to hurt you, ever."

Still, Olivia said nothing.

Vene sighed. "Dad said I should take responsibility for my decisions and how they affect you, and I'm trying to do just that. I didn't do anything to spite you, and I'm sorry I made you so angry—that wasn't my intention either. I . . ."

If she'd thought her mother didn't have the strength left to assert herself, she was wrong. Olivia held up her hand to stop Vene from talking.

"You have always lived your life in a selfish manner, Vene."

"No, I haven't!"

"Yes, yes, you have. It's not necessarily wrong."

"I don't feel selfish."

"There are reasons we become who we are, things that happened in the past that shape our future."

"Are you saying it's my fault we're not close? Well, maybe it is, but I stayed away because I always seemed to disappoint you. Not just now, but always. It gets old."

"That's not true. We are very different women, you and me. I have tried to accept that. As for Tony, he isn't my business. Dani is, Robert is . . ."

"Robert? What? How can my very ex-husband be your business? I married the wrong man, Mom. We had a child. I wanted to make it work, and I nearly bored myself to death trying. I'm sorry you liked him so much, but I wasn't going to waste my entire life faking it because of you. Or even for Dani, at the end of the day . . ." She stopped, her blood boiling. The more wound up she became, the calmer her mother appeared, and it only infuriated Vene more.

"Your daughter should be your priority in the same way you were mine. Robert is a good man. You were impatient with him."

"But I love Tony. In a way that I never, ever loved Robert. I married Robert because, frankly, you and Dad wanted me to. It made sense. He fit in. And I guess I wanted to fit in too. But my heart died a bit, even on our beautiful wedding day. I think I cried for all the wrong reasons that day, which is sinful." She felt tears coming and tried to suppress them, a lifelong habit. "I know it wasn't fair to Robert or to Dani who had no say, but I was miserable, Mom, truly lost. You don't like Tony because he's a dreamer, too romantic about life, you don't trust him, don't like his family. And now look . . . we dream together, we are building a life together that we are proud of—we're really happy, but you're not part of it. Why couldn't you have accepted him? Why can't you be happy for me?"

Those words were painful to say out loud, but she had kept quiet long enough. The cycle had to end, and end while there was still a chance for resolution.

"I'm getting cold now. I'd like to turn back," Olivia said.

"That's it? Conversation over? Why don't you just say it? That I should have stayed in the wrong marriage . . . just like you?"

"Enough, Vene. That's quite enough!" The look in her mother's eyes bordered on venomous.

Vene stood very still. She noticed her hands were balled up into fists. There was no way of getting through to her mother and get what she needed—approval for her choices. It was pathetic how much she wanted it. She wanted to forgive herself and her mother for all the ill feelings between them. She thought that if she could offer up some kind of reconciliation, her mother would gladly accept. But she should have known better.

"Fine," Vene replied as rudely as she could. ("Fuck you!" wasn't an option.) If she could have run down the hill and jumped in her car and left, she would have.

Roughly, she manhandled the wheelchair to get it to face downhill. It wasn't an easy maneuver. There wasn't a great deal of room on the path between the vines. One wheel got stuck on the uneven stones, so she yanked the chair backward, then pushed it forward again with extra force. Perhaps because it was too jerky a motion, perhaps her mother simply hadn't been holding on to the armrests properly, but to Vene's utter horror, the jolt pitched Olivia out of her seat and she landed hard on the dirt ground. Vene froze—then screamed.

"Oh my God! Mom! Oh my God, I'm so sorry! Mom . . . are you all right?!" She ran around the chair as fast as she could, terrified, mortified at what she'd done.

Her mother hadn't been able to brace herself for the fall. Her body was too thin and withered. The best she could do was cover her head before she hit the ground, taking most of the impact to her right hip. She groaned in pain. "Max . . . get Max," she managed to say.

"Here, Mom, I can help you." Vene tried to put her hand under her mother's armpit to lift her up.

"Don't! Don't touch me! Just get Max. Call him now."

Vene was beyond upset at what she had done, at all she had said. She didn't want to leave her mother there all alone, but Max would never hear her shouting from the top of these hills.

"Mom, I will be right back. I'm going to run and get help. I'll get Dad . . ."

"Not your father. No . . . listen to me . . . Max! Get Max," she groaned. She never wanted her husband when she was vulnerable, that much was clear. And she didn't want her daughter either. It would take more than just Max to lift her up, so Vene would have to ask the housekeeper and nurse to come. Anyone but family.

1946

Menu—discovering traditional meatballs

And the secret of my tomato sauce . . . finally!

Polpette in salsa di pomodoro

Linguine cacio e pepe

Profiteroles

Something happens to a body when it is free of stress and anxiety, Olivia thought, a profound openness and a sense of energy abounds. She'd spent so long feeling ashamed, struggling with her body's unwillingness to conceive, that she hadn't realized how closed off she'd become—until now. Just being in the same room as Victor gave her a sense of energy and peace. Instead of feeling nothing, she felt everything, and it was intoxicating. She felt like a woman again and it empowered her. For the first time in a long time, she believed she could do anything, be anything.

She cooked and gardened and discovered she had a talent for all aspects of the estate. Victor taught her about growing grapes: how to distinguish between the tastes and textures of each variety, how to choose which she preferred and why. In turn, her cooking was an expression of everything she felt for him. Jonathan was a million miles away. It seemed as though he never wanted to return, which was suiting her more and more.

She sat in the kitchen making notes in her cookbook. She had tried and failed to make Victor's mother's favorite recipe, traditional meatballs in tomato sauce, the way he liked them. It had become a joke between them. She checked her notes in the margins and realized the secret might lie in not manhandling the meat—over-manipulating the meatballs made them lose their fluffiness while cooking. And of course, there was the tomato sauce, the simplest of all things Italian but the most important. Give women the same ingredients all over the world, and an Italian mother's tomato sauce was still like no other.

Making these balls for the third time this week. Shaped them without suffocating them so they cook yet remain weightless—weeping juices when you cut through them. My pinch of magic this time was buttermilk used with the breadcrumbs. Will he notice? I picture them melting in his mouth . . . As for my heart . . .

She knew she was being hopelessly sentimental, but she didn't care. She began sketching in the top corner of the page, a chalice with a vine growing through it. Max entered the kitchen.

"Max, what do you think of this?" she asked, showing him her drawing. "Part of the label for our wine maybe?"

"It could be on the back perhaps," he replied, and began cleaning up the appalling mess she'd left.

"Why the back?" she demanded.

"The family name should be on the front, and I expect Mr. Winston would want it to look very simple."

"Yes, quite . . ." she replied, turning her attention back to her meatballs and combining all of the ingredients. She was missing eggs. She went to the pantry to forage for some when Victor suddenly slipped in behind her and shut the door. He spun her around and, before she could react, kissed her passionately, holding her tightly in his arms and ending their embrace with a dip.

"Heavens!" she whispered, wrapping her arms around his neck. "I didn't know you were such a good dancer."

"There are many things you don't know about me," he whispered with a smile.

"Secrets?" Olivia was intrigued.

"A few."

"I suppose we all have a few."

"I will tell you one of mine in exchange for one of yours."

Olivia had to think about this. The only two secrets she had both involved Victor.

"Okay," she said, "I'll play the game. I'll give you a hint, but you have to figure it out."

"Sounds interesting."

"Okay then. Here goes. I've only ever been in love once in my life."

"And . . . ?"

"And it's not with Jonathan." Oh my, she had said it. She felt her face flush red. She shut her eyes and looked away. Professing love to a man other than her husband, and before he spoke of his feelings for her—what was she thinking? She had said "I do" once before and only now realized she hadn't meant it—more like "I will." "I do" was about loving rather than obeying. Victor, she loved. She'd known it for a long time.

Victor turned her face back to him. He smiled at her.

"And what is your secret?" she asked shyly.

"That I want you to come with me to Italy. I can give you everything—I have a beautiful world there, beyond anything you could imagine. And the wine! What I plan to do with the Tuscan wine knowing what I know now. I can build it all, but I want you there. I need you there, by my side."

"I didn't know you had a vineyard of your own," was all she could blurt out. Move to Italy? Run away with Victor and leave everything behind? It seemed so impossible, but why not? Did she even want to stay? And wasn't her betrayal of Jonathan already unparalleled? Why stop now? Why not follow her heart all the way?

"I have more than just a vineyard. We are one of the largest landowners in Tuscany, but I have duties, an inheritance and a responsibility I ran away from. I have told you some of this, but the war is now over and there is hope again. Mussolini is dead. I am free, Olivia, free once more to dream. The fascists took so many lives, tore so many families apart, but we did not break, and I need to go back and help rebuild again. Come . . ." Victor looked imploringly at her. "Come with me. We can rebuild together."

Olivia buried her head in his chest. They stood in silence realizing how complicated their love made their lives. Victor broke away. "Come with me. Please, say you'll come."

Tears welled up in her eyes. "How? What about Jonathan?"

"Leave. You don't owe him your life. You don't even have family here—this is not your real home."

"It's the only home I have, Victor. My parents let go of me a long time ago and live on the other side of this country. Napa is all I have."

"No. You have me now . . . and I have Italy."

"I would destroy him by leaving," she whispered. "Do you have any idea how fragile this situation is?"

"He will survive."

"Not just Jonathan, our country! Everyone has a duty when the world explodes. He needs me for his work. He relies on me."

"That's ludicrous."

"I give him the security he needs at home to go off and do his work. This is what I agreed to, and everyone during the war made their own sacrifices. Why should I be any different?" She held his face between her hands. "Stay, stay here with me, and then we could still be together . . . Oh God . . . I don't know what I am doing . . ."

"Living, that's what you're doing. And for the first time in your life."

"He's a good man. He doesn't deserve to suffer." Reality had come crashing in on her affair, and she knew it. She averted her eyes as Victor stared down at her.

"He can't control you like that."

"I can't lose you, Victor, I can't," she said, increasingly upset.

"You don't have to. I will look after you. You also deserve the things you want. Come with me. It's not so tragic, Olivia. It's not as if you have children together."

Instinctively, Olivia slapped him across the face. Victor had unwittingly unleashed her other secret, and she hadn't been able to help herself.

He didn't flinch. "Forget about believing in me—what is tragic is you not believing in yourself." Victor left the pantry and slammed the door, leaving her in darkness once more.

chapter thirteen

1996

The damage had been done. Years ago, in fact, but the bruises now on Olivia's body seemed to Vene to be a visual reminder of what happened when they tried to communicate. After the fall that day, Olivia didn't have the strength to go out for fresh air for the whole of the following week. A tumble like that in her state could have broken every bone in her body, and she insisted on staying in bed most hours.

Loss of mobility was a genuine setback in her small world where even showering on her own was a huge achievement. Before the fall, Max and Jonathan had convinced her to start taking at least some of her meals downstairs, believing that a change of atmosphere would do her some good, and she had indeed been a bit better. But now her appetite had gone from small to nearly nonexistent despite Max cooking her favorite foods every day. Sadness and fear crept back into everyone's conversation, a forlorn reckoning that she might not be around for much longer.

As for Vene, every time she retreated from her mother's bedroom, she felt ever more unsettled. To compensate, she buried herself in her mother's cookbooks, reading every page of every book, searching for clues as to what created her defenses to keep the world at bay. Every instinct told Vene there was a reason why her mother was so shut down—it couldn't be lack of love or care because she had both; it had to be something else. Her recipes proved a passion for the food she was cooking, and yet that passion was nowhere to be seen in her everyday life. Vene certainly had never seen it and was almost resigned to the fact that she never would.

Tony had been extremely understanding about her need to stay longer and called her every night to check in. "How did it go today? Any changes?" he asked.

"Nope, nothing. She's not talking much either. Every time I go in there, she looks up at me briefly and then either goes back to sleep or watches TV or something. Definitely no room to talk about stuff right now," she replied.

"Well, that's normal for her. She's so weak, Vene, you've got to remember life is just exhausting for her. When my dad was sick last year, the most exciting thing he could do was get up to go to the bathroom. It's just the way it will be from now on."

"I know that, of course I know that. She hardly does anything and is completely spent. And the bruises . . . Oh God, like I needed to see those . . ."

"That's harsh."

"No, I mean, I already walk around with a huge sense of guilt without being reminded of an actual reason to feel guilty."

"Why do you feel guilty? Aside from pushing your mother down a dirt hill."

"Very funny." She walked over to the wine rack and pulled out a 1990 Chateau Margaux. She uncorked it and poured herself a big glass. Gotta love Napa—wine was the answer to every problem. She swirled it around her glass and inhaled the rich smell: cassis, truffle, and violets. She took a long sip and sat down again. "We don't have the tools to communicate, I suppose. And I blame myself for not being able to find them. She's my mother, Tony. I know she loves me, but I just don't think she likes me very much, and I must have done something to cause that. I've felt this way for such a long time. Our dynamic is so unnatural."

"Do you like her?"

It was a fair question to which she had no answer.

She picked up the cookbook and flipped once again to the back. "There's a quote written down in Italian. What does '*Nel vino c'è la verità*' mean?"

"'In wine, there is truth.'"

She took another sip. "Yep. Once you start drinking wine, only the truth comes out of your mouth." She paused. "I wonder why she wrote that?"

"She's a wine producer; her life was about wine. So the truth of her life started there, I guess."

"I suppose," she said, flipping through the book again. "But why all the anger? Disappointment? Was it the effects of the war? Maybe she wanted more children, like I did, and felt a sense of loss. Oh my God, maybe we share that sense of loss and I never knew?" There was only so far she would go with Tony on this subject. It was his loss too, as he had reminded her a few times already, and she wasn't alone in the regret.

"She doesn't seem angry. Or lost," he said.

"Tony, she hates you for no reason. That's not normal."

"She doesn't hate me."

Vene was silent.

"She hates me?" Tony questioned.

Wine makes you say things you regret, she thought. "No, I'm exaggerating," she lied. "She just never wanted to get too involved with you, or our life together. She still talks to Robert."

"Seriously? Why would she still talk to Robert?"

"Maybe because of Dani. Who knows? Who cares. But it's just another thing that gets between us."

"Vene, your mother and I have our own understanding. No more, no less than a polite acknowledgement of each other's position. I'm okay with that. She is the matriarch of the estate and I am the Italian that swept her daughter off her feet. We couldn't be more different but we respect each other's place."

"Yeah, and unfortunately for you, she'd put you in the stables with the other stallions." Tony made a weird horse-like sound and she had to laugh. "I am lucky you're so accommodating. I'm not sure I would be if I were in your shoes. She's pretty rude to you and you don't deserve it."

"She's conventional. Besides, I'm not married to her. I'm married to you. Don't worry about it."

"Listen to this," Vene said, "she wrote this on the page of an eggplant parmesan recipe."

I pour my heart into the eggplant as a distraction today
trying not to look into his eyes for fear of being seen.

"The way she writes about her heart, it's on nearly every page. It's like I'm reading a romance novel, only I just can't picture it being about her and Dad. They were married so young. So many of her thoughts seemed newly formed." She turned more pages. "And she writes about desserts melting in her mouth as if love itself had a taste. Passionate pleas mixed with agony and remorse. How the heck can spaghetti with meatballs or osso buco be so torturous?"

"Especially when no one knew she was cooking," Tony added.

"Maybe it was because no one knew who she really was—what she was really feeling. How lonely that must have been. Having it all and yet not feeling complete. I can't imagine my father was sensitive to much of that."

"Sounds like she was dealing with a lot more than hiding in the kitchen. Was all of it written a long time ago?"

"Yeah, I think so. It would have been the forties and before I was born. I saw a photo of them; it's on the back cover of the coffee table book. They looked like totally different people. What was she trying to say?"

The question had time to linger.

Then she added, "I think Jenny and my father were having an affair."

"Really?" Tony asked, sounding curious.

"They were always together, so close. From the beginning, way back, she was always there. And even now, seeing them together on his birthday. There are definitely notes in the cookbooks about pained hearts, and my guess is that my mother found out and was shattered."

"That's a big conclusion, although it would explain a lot if it were true."

"I'm not someone she would ever confide in, but I would love to know what really went on because you're right, it would then explain a lot."

"Or not. Maybe these secrets have been locked away for good reason. It could be detrimental to everyone to have them all come out."

"Perhaps . . ." she said, unconvinced.

"She's dying, and you need to figure out how you're going to say goodbye. For you, and for her."

Vene knew he was right. If she continued to focus on all that was wrong with her mother, she would never get anywhere. Reconciliation came from forgiveness and acceptance, even if you couldn't fully comprehend the "why" of it all. Still, it was easy to say. She had flashbacks of childhood moments where she found herself alone, hitting her pillow in frustration. The time she ran away and no one had even noticed. The time she sent hate mail to her parents when they left her alone to travel abroad. All those times she lay on the grass between the vines feeling overwhelmed by the emptiness of the sky. The only child with no one to play with. But now she wondered if her mother had been lonely too.

She swirled the wine around her glass and watched the rich color slowly fade down the sides.

"I miss you," she said.

"I miss you too," he replied.

"I think you should come. I didn't before, but I think it's too long to go without seeing each other. I don't know how long I'm going to be here. I wanted to leave, but then I'd only feel like I should come back."

"I know."

"But I need to see you."

"I know."

"You make me feel calm."

"I know."

The doorbell rang. It was too late for any visitors, and the staff had gone to bed.

"Oh God, the doorbell. I need to go," she said, not wanting to hang up. She could hear her father in his study as she walked to the front door. He called out, curious to see who was there at that time of night. Any ring of the bell those days was infrequent and unexpected, and nighttime was saved for only the doctor or the night nurse. "I better go, Tony, love you."

"Love you too. Night," he said, and hung up.

She opened the door. To her shock, Tony stood there, brandishing an enormous mobile phone.

"I was just passing by . . ." he said, grinning.

Vene nearly burst into tears. "Cool looking phone," she managed.

"Took it from the production. Got time for a quickie?"

"Oh, Tony . . ." She wrapped her arms around him and pulled him in tight. Her whole body still tingled when he touched her—he had a way with her that was all his. His smell alone made her want him. He kissed her lips and her neck, then nibbled her ears.

"Everything okay out there?" Jonathan called out. "Vene? Who's at the door?"

She giggled like a naughty teenager. "Don't worry, Dad. I got it." She quietly led Tony into the house and snuck him up the stairs—two young lovers again, corridor creeping.

1946

Menu to calm a mind

Busy cooking, flavorful and easier than expected

Zuppa di pesce

Haricots frits

Fromage

Victor stayed away all week, and Olivia didn't go after him. After having a million conversations with him in her mind, she was no closer to knowing what to do. The question remained—could the fantasy they'd been living ever become her reality?

She tried to calm herself by cooking, making soups and stew with Max—the two of them, eating alone together. Every day she brought in green beans, carrots, and squash straight from her garden. Planting and harvesting food, there was something primal about the process, a feeling of contribution. Max had seemed unusually quiet as well the last few days, and several of their meals were spent in near silence. But tonight, while Olivia was watching Max prepare the fish soup—a favorite of his mother's, he'd told her—she felt the need for conversation. She realized that she didn't know much about Max's personal life, even though he was privy to all sorts of her own secrets.

"Where are your parents from again, Max?" she asked as she cleaned and chopped the vegetables.

"A small fishing village called Monterosso," he replied. "It is in the north, on the coast. Part of a group of five villages called Cinque Terre. Both my parents were born there," he added, washing the grit from the mussels.

"And what did your father do?"

"My father was a fisherman, as was his father and grandfather before him, and my mother grew many crops: olives, lemons, even grapes. It is very beautiful there."

"Sounds it."

Max started to simmer the garlic in oil and butter, adding thyme, red pepper, fennel seed, and bay leaf. He used saffron and tomato paste as well, reflecting the flavor of the soups made in central Italy. There was a distinction in ingredients depending on what part of Italy the recipe came from. Northern Italy had notably heavier dishes due to the colder weather: a preference for using butter over olive oil, Bolognese sauce from Bologna, the white truffles of Alba, risotto from Piedmont, not to mention the north's staple dish of polenta. The south was notorious for their seafood and, of course, pesto: garlic, basil, pine nuts, and olive oil. Max added a generous glug of dry white wine and some stock and let the sauce cook for a bit. "I used to spend many afternoons on the beach watching the fishing boats come back. The waters could be rough, and the entire village would gather round to help and see what was the catch of the day. The air was very salty and warm like the water most of the time, and we lived very close to one another, cut into the mountainside. We left long before the war, but one day I would love to go back. One day when Italy is strong again." Olivia had to stop herself from picturing her Italian life with Max there too. Was it possible? Could it work?

She poured herself and Max some wine. They were drinking a dry chardonnay produced by her neighbors, the Taylor family. The Taylors had been in Napa for years, originally as farmers, and this was their first attempt at chardonnay. It went extremely well with the spice and herbs of the fish soup. It was a relief, almost a reprieve, to get out of her own head for once. She was grateful that Max felt unusually talkative.

"So why Napa?"

"My mother had met a woman from the next village who had visited California. All she spoke of was oranges and grapes and fields of gold flowers. It was everything we had but much more. Many Italians had left for the coast of California after the Gold Rush to find their own riches. We weren't going to be alone there."

"So it was your mother who brought the family to America? That was incredibly brave of her. I'm impressed."

Max laid the marinated fish, mussels, clams, and lemons in a heavy-bottomed pan and slowly poured the heated broth on top. "The railway had been built to connect the villages some years back, and it made it easier to travel to Roma. It gave people a chance to dream about going to other places. Most didn't, but my parents did." The clams and mussels were slowly opening. How beautiful it was to watch and smell. "My father was a successful anchovy fisherman, but his dream was to teach. He was a talker and a thinker. He heard about an opportunity from his cousin in San Francisco, also a fisherman and doing very well there. He thought he could fish during the day and study at night at a California university. So he moved us all the way to America."

Olivia couldn't help but identify with Max's story—was it a sign for her to leave? Other people had a desire for a life beyond what they knew. Other people took a leap of faith. She looked up. There was water damage on the ceiling above their heads, a few darkened, yellow spots in a circular shape. She wondered if she would live here long enough to worry about fixing it.

"And then what happened? Did he become a teacher?" She liked to think that Max's father had done well.

"No. He is still a fisherman who thinks and writes a lot. Poetry, mostly. And my mother cooks. They opened a small Italian restaurant in Fisherman's Wharf, and I grew up smelling of fish and tomato sauce."

"And your brother? What does he do now?"

"He's the one who went to university. Made my father happy to live out his dreams through his own son."

Olivia wondered whether he felt resentment or resignation. Max wasn't an academic, and his life—much like his mother's, it seemed—had revolved around the kitchen and running a house. His dedication to his work and expertise had always been exemplary, and she hoped he never felt like a disappointment to them. Her own parents lived across the country in Connecticut and called twice a year. She felt no obligation to them. They'd seemed happy enough to marry her off into another family, and they kept in touch with awkward conversations once a month at best. And now she could taste a new future, and her heart raced at the thought of leaving Napa. She could see the childhood boy in Max as he stirred the pot and let the ingredients settle, wiping his stained hands on his white apron. He always kept his emotions in check, but there was definitely a sadness to him—like a boy who had lost his favorite toy boat down a river, not realizing it would be gone forever. Max was a great chef, a great houseman, and they were truly lucky to have him. She wondered what dreams he'd abandoned and if any still lingered. He was still young enough to hope, wasn't he?

"Cinque Terre . . . sounds romantic and idyllic. I'd love to go there one day," she said.

"It was bombed in the war, my village. There was a lot of damage. Many men there fought for the Resistance. Families were divided. Much of Italy has changed since we left. But yes, beautiful."

"Did you lose family too?"

"Everyone lost someone."

"Of course," she said. Victor too had told her how his family and friends had suffered while their country had been in the grip of Il Duce. She looked at Max. His face was kind and full of life. Olivia had come to rely on the comfort he gave her. Listening to his stories reminded her that life promised change. It was almost too scary, too exciting to contemplate for real, but she knew she needed to make the biggest of decisions soon.

The clams and mussels were fully opened now, and dinner was ready. Olivia raised her glass to Max. "*Saluti alla vita*," she said.

"To life," Max said, and clinked his glass to hers.

chapter fourteen

1996

The blessing of a small town was how connected you felt when something good or bad happened: when someone was born or someone died. The cycle of life felt like the seasons—natural, predictable, a few surprises to be sure, but basically there was a comfort in knowing things were as they should be. In Napa, the community made you feel as though you had a place in other people's lives.

Olivia was known all over the valley, not just in Yountville. She had been on the city council, the arts council, and sold a large part of her produce at the oldest Napa Valley grocer in Oakville. Every year they gave her a special stand to celebrate the "Winston Family Victory Garden" planted during wartime efforts. Everywhere Vene went, in fact, there was another reminder of her mother's influence, another person who wanted to send her their love.

Before Tony drove back to LA, they went together to the Oakville Grocery for their favorite coffee ritual. Built in 1881, the grocery had always been a central hub for winemakers and farmers. There were black-and-white photos of Napa on the shelves, reminding the local customers of their heritage. Vene was standing in line when she noticed that the man paying at the counter was her old gynecologist, someone she'd hoped to never see again. She noted he still wore those odd Timberland-looking shoes with his posh suit and how he now had hardly any hair. She was immediately reminded of two things: one, she hadn't had a mammogram or checkup in well over a year, and two, he was the doctor who'd performed her abortion nearly ten years ago. Watching him pay for his latte made her feel a bit sick. Tony must have read her face because he looked at her quizzically. "You okay?"

Had she known that having that abortion would set her on a different path for the rest of her life she never, ever, would have gone through with it. Of course no woman thinks she'll never get pregnant again, especially when getting pregnant came so easily. She'd been weak and hated herself for destroying what should have been a celebration of true love. She remembered so clearly her mother telling her to get rid of it. *It!* The decision had seemed shockingly easy for her—they'd discussed it for twenty minutes, tops. Then the drive to that doctor's office, the numbness that followed, still palpable after all these years. Hindsight was only painful when regret was involved.

Standing there, she found herself caressing her stomach, letting it out instead of the usual conscious suck-in. It relaxed into a round ball shape under her hand. She was wearing her big jeans, the ones she wore that had some breathing room, and her tummy pushed against the top button. Although she was forty-nine and probably perimenopausal, she nearly felt and looked a few months pregnant. The slight ache in her back . . . the heightened emotions she felt . . . even her breasts felt tender. How extraordinary that would have been! Ha! Was it even possible? She let herself linger on that thought until the doctor finished paying and turned toward them to get his sugar.

"Excuse me," he said, smiling politely at Vene and Tony, just two people blocking the sugar stand. It was fitting that he didn't recognize her even though she'd been his patient for years. She had directed all her misplaced anger over the abortion at this man and had never gone back to see him again.

She stepped out of the way and ordered their coffees while Tony took a seat outside. Needing a minute to recover, she was grateful Tony had walked away. He was a devoted stepfather to Dani and would have loved to have a child together, but he'd never seemed too worried by her inability to give him one. She wasn't damaged to him the way she was to herself. Tony came from a big Italian family dominated by strong, loving, earthy women. He was raised amongst a lot of chaos and a lack of privacy that he was only too happy not to replicate. Vene was an only child, as was her mother. On her father's side, she had two aunts living on the East Coast: one who never had kids and one who had two much older boys. No one ever came to visit. Growing up, her immediate family was just that, very immediate, slap-you-in-the-face immediate. Just the three of them. And Max. When she was younger, she remembered being asked why she started playing with make-believe friends. She figured out it wasn't control issues or primal sadness or some sort of strange social dysfunction. It was because she was lonely. Somewhere along the way she thought she'd eventually have loads of kids herself—make her own big, messy, chaotic family so she would never have to feel that way again.

She went outside. The chill in the air was bracing. She found Tony sitting at a communal table, which was telling—she would have instinctively chosen a two-top, while he was used to the shared experience. Inside of her there was a struggle brewing. She was grateful Tony came but also relieved he was going back to LA because her moods at that moment—whether fired up by grief, anxiety, or plain old middle-aged hormones—were hard to explain to him, let alone herself.

She smiled at the random people at their table, quickly putting on sunglasses to discourage conversation.

"What's going on with you?" Tony asked.

"Nothing."

"Vene?"

"What? Nothing. This place just has so many memories for me."

"Yeah." He took her hand across the table, rubbing his thumb over the top of her fingers to warm her up. She kept her hand on his and smiled at him warmly. Tony had always saved her from herself. She would have never had the courage to leave her life—her very unsatisfying life—if she hadn't fallen that hard for someone. He'd made her believe that another path was possible.

"I dreamed a lot here about what life would look like when I grew up. And then all of a sudden, I did grow up, and it's weird being back here knowing that a big chunk of my life is now behind me."

"You're not that old."

"But it's true. We spend so much time saying, 'One day, I'm going to do this or that . . .' and for us, that one day is now. We should live our lives knowing that."

"I would say we do. Maybe not always, but we've never waited."

"No, we haven't. But I'm not so sure my mother didn't get caught out waiting. Every time I think of her, I picture someone unhappy."

"That's depressing."

"Yeah, it's a waste." She put her other hand on his. "I started living when I met you."

"Same. And I'm sorry about your mom," he added. "This is not going to be easy for a while, you know that, right?"

"When has it ever been easy between me and my mom? I think she might actually appreciate having her reception here, instead of the house. This place is forever celebrating her."

"Her funeral?" Tony asked.

"Why not? Everyone loves coming here. They all know her; they practically have her name on a perma-plaque above the fruit and veg section. They sell our wine . . . it's perfect."

"How about we just have some coffee right now and worry about the funeral a bit later," he said gently.

"She's dying, Tony, and we may as well plan things now. Maybe I should ask her?" It was matter-of-fact, but she knew her mother would appreciate the sentiment.

"Why don't you speak to your father first? I'm sure he will have strong opinions about it all."

"Or not. For all the strength of character my dad has, he seems completely adrift when it comes to my mom. He has no idea how to connect with her. He arranged for the nursing staff to stay round the clock because she's dying, but I think it's so he can avoid her as well. He sits with her every day chatting about news headlines and bits of local gossip, but other than that, he spends most of his time in his study or on walks around the property. I really only see him for meals."

"He's probably incredibly sad. And maybe even scared."

She took a sip of her coffee. "Or guilty . . ." she added dryly.

1946

Menu for the war efforts

Best bite-size delights and cup of soup idea

Zuppa di pomodoro con olio al basilico

Parmigiana di melanzane

Gnocchi di zucca butternut

Throughout the war, Napa Valley remained agriculturally productive. With shortages in the labor force due to locals serving in the armed forces, nervous wine producers were forced to be proactive. The Napa Farm Production Committee came up with a plan that promised top wages and extra gasoline, something that was being rationed, to ensure their harvests. In 1942, the American government also started a program called Los Braceros to help alleviate the shortage of manpower in farms across the US. This program recruited able and willing Mexican men to come to America as temporary wartime laborers. A significant number of these men stayed on after the war, and some still worked at the Winston Estate. In addition, in 1945, 250 prisoner-of-war German soldiers also made their mark in Napa, rescuing a prune and tomato crop. At first the locals were unsure of these men. There was serious talk amongst almost everyone living in Napa as to whether they could stomach having the Germans on their land. But soon they realized that the presence of these men—albeit through a strange set of circumstances—wasn't something to fear, and an odd sense of basic humanity prevailed. Napa's harvests had always been fruitful, and 1946 was no exception.

To celebrate the post-wartime boom, an event was held in Yountville, and Olivia was asked to participate with both the Winston wine and her vegetables. She had entered a few local competitions with some prodding from Max and won several awards for her artichokes and green beans. Max encouraged her to make some Italian dishes to showcase the season's squash and eggplant, and Victor was meant to come and present their wine tastings. Table wine was becoming very popular in America as more and more people drank wine with their meals and not just for religious or special occasions.

Olivia was desperate to see Victor and thought she could use the event to be with him, albeit publicly. He had stayed clear of the house and her for over a week now, and it was driving her crazy. Did he not understand the turmoil she felt as she weighed her choices? Jonathan and Napa were all that she'd known so far in her short, sheltered life. She had roots here, and an opportunity to make this place a success. This was the first home she had built, her first attempt at belonging somewhere. The fact that she blamed Jonathan for her barren body meant that maybe she'd never given him the chance he deserved. She could change that. He was a good man, an honest man. If he really understood her passion for cooking and could see how far she'd come, he would accept her role in the kitchen and be proud of her, and their relationship might improve. She knew he loved her as fully as he knew how, and she felt deeply for him too, she told herself. She knew it was wrong and shameful to indulge in fantasy that could destroy a marriage, and at the end of the day, loyalty and duty meant something to her; she was a diplomat's wife, after all.

But then there was everything else—feelings that had nothing to do with shame or blame, loyalty or title, but rather life's purest emotion . . . love. How could she deny herself that? She ached thinking about Victor. The idea of turning the corner and seeing him put her in a constant state of alert. She felt almost nauseous with arousal. She dreamed of Victor every night and woke each day wanting to see his face. Was love always so sensuous?

She was in the kitchen packing up the food to take to Yountville when the door opened. She spun around, only to find Max.

"Mrs. Winston, I already loaded the car with the baskets of artichokes. We can put the cooked food into these boxes and lay them down in the back."

Olivia helped him stack the boxes. "Do you think Victor is meeting us there, or shall we wait for him here?" she said, willing him to tell her that Victor was coming.

"He's meeting us there," Max replied matter-of-factly, heading to the car with his load.

Olivia stood smiling a huge and wonderful smile knowing she would soon see Victor. She had imagined so many times what their new life might look like. In the hills in Italy, looking out at a sprawling horizon; in a boat on a lake, Victor rowing with that crooked smile on his face she'd come to love. Or dancing in his arms, twirling around, her face buried in his neck, his sweet scent all around her. In a country kitchen, the smell of fresh herbs and spices in the air, she in her apron humming, Victor pouring the wine. This was the life that lay in front of her, there for the taking. If only she had the courage to grab hold.

It was a crisp, golden day. The sort of fall day where every color was highlighted against the sky. As Max and Olivia arrived at the marketplace, the stands were just beginning to fill out. There was a lot of commotion: farmers and winemakers mingling, tables being set up for tastings with baskets of fruits and vegetables decorating each stall. The greenest of beans, big red and yellow peppers, a rainbow of carrots—purple, orange, and white, mirroring the colors of the hills.

Max found their spot next to the Mondavi stand where many Italians worked. He enjoyed his time speaking in his native tongue, and in Napa there were plenty of Italian immigrants who felt the same. Olivia always took note of how animated he became speaking in Italian and how passionate the exchanges were. In fact, most wine producers they knew had some connection to Italy. The Mondavis themselves were from Sassoferrato, central Italy, and had moved to the US as newlyweds. They'd lived in Minnesota before coming to California and started a shipping company that sold wine grapes until they moved to Napa, ultimately buying the Charles Krug Winery a few years back.

Olivia began taking her food out of the containers: little individual paper doilies filled with bite-size gnocchi, small portions of eggplant parmesan, and paper cups filled with tomato soup and a parmesan crostini. Her intention was to share the food as a celebration of the times, and her incredible victory garden, but it also wasn't lost on anyone how much better their wine tasted when paired with Italian food. Olivia nodded and smiled to various townspeople as she scanned the crowds for Victor—just the thought of him made her beam.

She finished the last of the platters and began arranging the tablecloth just so when she felt something and glanced up. He was standing about twenty feet away. The crowds of people faded from her line of vision. He walked toward her, and she held on to the edge of the table to resist running into his arms. He stopped as he reached her and held her gaze. Then he leaned forward and put the purple flower he was holding in her hair. She touched it and blushed. She was acutely aware they were in public with potential eyes on them, but he didn't seem to care.

"I've missed you," he said.

"I've missed you too," she whispered back.

"*Sei bellissima* . . . You look beautiful."

"I look exhausted. But thank you." She hadn't slept well in days. They stood there without speaking. "Max packed the cases of wine in the back of the car," she said eventually. "'I can help you get them," she added with a coy smile.

"I'll go, you stay. You wouldn't want anyone wondering why

you're following me." He left just as Helen Winter, a neighbor and fellow wine producer, came up to the stall.

"Hello, love," Helen said.

The two women kissed cheeks. "Hello, Helen," Olivia said, feeling relieved that Victor had gone. She didn't trust Helen.

"Mother Nature was good to all of us this year. The grapes and of course your vegetables are always so delicious. What's this?" Helen pointed at the gnocchi. "May I?"

"Of course, please. It has butternut squash inside."

"You know that's my favorite." She popped the whole thing in her mouth, then moaned. "Oh, divine. Olivia, you are so talented. My victory garden is more like a lost garden. Everything looks shriveled compared to yours."

"Don't be silly."

"No, I mean it, you're so good. And your food! Jonathan is a lucky man."

"It's mostly Max. I don't cook much when Jonathan's around. You know, it's more about entertaining when he's home than cooking. It's just a hobby, something I do infrequently to pass the time while he's away." Helen was a friend, a good friend, but still, Olivia felt it prudent to keep the extent of her cooking a secret.

"Well, I say he's a foolish man to keep you away from the kitchen. I'm going to tell him that when I see him next."

"Oh, please don't," Olivia said a little too vehemently. Then she added, "Honestly, he really does have a problem with me cooking. It's ridiculous, I know, but . . ."

"Say no more. Mum's the word. If Martin knew I liked to gamble, I think he'd divorce me!"

"Gamble?" Olivia was caught off guard.

"Horses, cards, you name it, I just love it. It's the thrill of it all. I'm just so bored sometimes, and well, I don't know, it gives me excitement. Lord knows we all need a little action around here."

"And so he doesn't know about any of it?" Olivia asked curiously.

Helen leaned into the table. "There's a lot Martin doesn't know. After three kids in five years, I feel as though I'm drowning half the time. Where did my life go? You've been smart to wait. He's gone most days, and I'm barely coping by myself with the children. I meet up with a few other women, and when we can, we sneak out to the Sonoma County Fairgrounds and bet the horses or play cards for money. I know we shouldn't, but frankly, it's so much fun. More than I've had with Martin in a long time. Probably shouldn't admit that out loud, but we girls have to stick together, right? You should join us sometime, but not a word to Jonathan. Promise?"

"Promise." Secrets and lies. Everyone had secrets and lies.

Helen took another gnocchi and gobbled it down just as Victor approached.

"It's good, isn't it?" Victor said to Helen.

Helen covered her mouth with her hand. "Mmmm, delicious. Divine!"

Victor smiled at Olivia. He was standing close enough for her to touch, but she dared not. It took all her self-control not to lean her head against him.

"You should taste her pomodoro sauce. Better than my mother's, and that is saying a lot," Victor said.

Trying not to blush, Olivia pulled herself together. "Helen, this is Victor Viandanti, our incredible winemaker from Italy. Victor, this is Mrs. Winter, a good friend of mine from the valley."

Victor bowed his head respectfully. This time, Olivia noticed, it was Helen who was trying not to blush.

"Pleasure to meet you, Mrs. Winter," Victor said.

"Helen, please call me Helen," Helen replied, and shot Olivia a schoolgirl look of envy.

"Of course—Helen." He smiled, and Olivia watched Helen glow in response.

She knew exactly what Helen was thinking about Victor. Helen began endlessly discussing the season's grapes with him, nervously talking a mile a minute, giving far too many details away about how her husband was trying to cut corners, where their winemaker had decided to buy their grapes from and the prices they were paying. She even talked about what Mrs. Mondavi had worn to their house for dinner last week, anything to just keep Victor's attention. Little did she know that all the while Victor had linked his index finger around Olivia's pinky under the table. Shock waves went through her body. *Oh, Helen, if you only knew . . .*

chapter fifteen

1996

During the long days languishing around the house, it occurred to Vene that her father might not have a desire to live alone on the estate. Even surrounded by staff, he would be by himself. She pictured him at the dining table with only the newspaper for company, or having a Scotch in his study, smoking his pipe by the window on his own. She understood that Max baked bread more for her mother than her father, and she wondered if the house would simply smell vacant and stale after her mother's death. She imagined her father ambling around the property with his walking stick, bending down to pick some flowers and then realizing there was no one inside to give them to. She saw him smaller, an older man sleeping in their king-sized bed, taking up one side, one pillow, leaving a single dent in the mattress.

What would happen to the estate? Would he sell it? Would she be expected to move back in and help run things? Her father's financial partners owned 51 percent of the label. It was they who made all the important decisions now. The estate itself was really a beautiful money pit that no longer made a whole lot of sense for their family to own. None of these issues had ever been discussed before her mother became ill, and now they were living with a moratorium on all decision-making, except what to eat for dinner. There was never the right moment to consider or debate the future while they were so painfully stuck in the present.

There was a knock on the side kitchen door. Jonathan was in his study, Max in his room after cleaning up dinner, and Vene wasn't expecting anyone. It was too late surely for local visitors, and besides they would have used the front door. Even her mother's nurses had made their shift change. She heard the door open and then softly close again. She crept to the top of the stairs and watched as Jenny walked into the hallway, put her handbag and coat down on the table, placing flowers down beside them before heading to the study. How had she gotten in? Did she have a key? The familiarity was odd to see, as was the touching up of her hair before she pushed the study door open. Once again, Vene couldn't dismiss the idea. Would Jenny finally take her mother's seat at the table once she was gone?

Vene could have shut her door and gone back to reading herself to an early sleep, but she wanted to spy on her eighty-seven-year-old father and his seventy-something-year-old friend. It was ridiculous, really. She crept downstairs and stood in front of the closed door. She could hear laughter through the thick oak. How many times, she wondered, had they met for a nightcap? Or for something else? She felt no resentment, just sadness that she couldn't remember the last time her mother had really laughed with or without her father. She listened for a few more minutes. It didn't sound as though they were having an intimate conversation, so she opened the door with a quick knock beforehand.

"Vene," Jonathan said calmly, "come in, come in." Instead of being surprised, he seemed . . . oddly natural, sitting in his chair, plush burgundy leather with comfortable armrests, while Jenny held a brandy opposite him in her mother's chair—the one with the Asian patterns in red-and-cream silk. Vene's first thought when faced with the cozy tableau in front of her was to back out of the room. But instead she joined them, pulling up a chair next to her father and pouring herself a drink.

"Cheers." She smiled at Jenny, trying to read all the nuances of the moment. Jenny returned the smile and then clinked glasses with Jonathan. Vene wasn't sure what she was trying to uncover, but neither her father nor Jenny appeared to feel remotely ill at ease.

"Dad, Dani is doing a paper in school about post–World War II relations with Russia and the beginning of the Cold War. I told her she could speak with you, if that's okay."

"Is there a specific angle she's focusing on?"

"Italy—the fall of Mussolini and then the aftermath. Something about the Italian reparations that never got made in the Paris deal . . . not really sure."

Jenny interrupted. "That was when you went to that conference just after the war. End of summer, '46. You had that terrible flu and you tried sending someone else, but Byrnes wasn't having it."

"Who's Byrnes?" Vene asked.

"James Byrnes, secretary of state," Jonathan replied. "It was a peace conference with France, the UK, the US, and the Soviets primarily, to discuss the aftermath of the war: monetary reparations, territory adjustments, that sort of thing. It went on and on for months. We were trying to have agreements before the official conference the following year. The Soviets were terrible to deal with."

"Your father was masterful, it should be said. I always thought it was largely because of his efforts that they were able to move forward with the Paris conference the following year," Jenny added, looking admiringly at Jonathan.

"Slight exaggeration," Jonathan said.

"Not really," Jenny protested, taking a sip of her drink.

Watching their banter convinced Vene that whatever was going on between her father and Jenny, they were intimate, and unaware how easily others could tell. They had the sort of closeness that comes from really knowing a person.

"That might be a good starting point for Dani," Jonathan said.

"What point?" Vene had lost track of their conversation.

"The Paris Peace Conference of '46."

"Yes, great. A lot going on in the forties for you, it seems. You were away a lot."

"The war ended. My work was very consuming. I traveled nearly every month back then," Jonathan explained.

"Did you enjoy it? The travel?" Vene asked.

"It was exciting. Rewarding."

"And Mom?" Vene hadn't missed his glance at Jenny. "Did she stay here all the while?"

"She wasn't exactly without things to do. She had the vineyard, and then she had you. And we had moved to London by then." Whether Jonathan was doing it on purpose or not, he stared at his daughter as if challenging her next comment before she made it. Was history rewriting itself right here in this room? Vene wondered.

"Right. Well, I am sure you have stories you can't find so easily in books written about those times. About your work, that is. There must be hundreds I don't even know about. Have you written any of this down? Sounds like there might be a book in there?"

"I've been telling him that for years," Jenny agreed, lightly.

"I'm sure," Vene said, surprising even herself with her sarcastic tone. They were sounding like a married couple.

Jonathan cleared his throat. "I thought I was too old and tired to start. But I did begin to go back to my notes I kept at the time, in my black book. I used to take that thing with me everywhere. Reading annotations from meetings and such gives some insight, some history. Who had the strongest handshake . . . lots of details. I'll show them to Dani when she's here next."

Vene imagined him writing down his notes on his political agendas, ideas, and insights into personalities, observations made behind closed doors. She pictured her mother in the kitchen just on the other side of the same walls, scribbling away about life, food, and love. Two people living side by side in two separate worlds, sharing emotions through only pen and paper.

"When did you stop? When we came back from London?" Vene asked. "When postwar America entered the hippie movement? Hopefully you took a lot of notes about that—those must have been colorful times."

He looked at Jenny. Jenny looked down at her lap. An oddly uncomfortable silence stung the air. Perhaps one question too far? "I should be going. I only came for a quick hello to see how you were doing," Jenny said.

At nine o'clock at night? Vene wanted to comment, but thought otherwise.

"No, Jenny, please stay, finish your drink. I was just going to make myself some tea and get an early night." Vene rose and gave her father a kiss on the cheek and did the same to Jenny before either could argue.

In the kitchen she waited for the kettle to boil. She pulled out her mother's cookbook and moved her hands over the cover in a circular motion, as if to conjure up its secrets. As an only child, she had only her own memories to fill in the blanks over the years. How had her parents loved each other? The formality of their relationship, their mutual respect, answered surface questions, but it was becoming increasingly clear that how they chose to live as husband and wife wasn't as straightforward as she'd once believed. The book between her hands was a tale of discovery—a love triangle perhaps? A diary of a diplomat's wife and her troubled heart.

Parmigiana di melanzane—I planted these
eggplants with every ounce of love I had left inside
myself for him—and then baked it perfectly.
But he never once looked up while he ate.

Astice al vapore—I steamed these beautiful creatures, adding only lemon, a splash of wine, and a little butter to the pan. Then we tore them apart, licking the juices from our lips. Worth every bite. Fall 1946

She knew her father was allergic to shellfish. Why did she date this entry? Her father was away so much of the time; her mother must have had an entire life that existed during his absence. Who could blame her? Women just didn't speak of their private lives back in the day, but surely it would be wrong to assume they didn't have one. And then there was her father, so at ease with his relationship with Jenny . . .

It was a lot to think about. And yet it had nothing to do with her own need to set the record straight with her mother. Or did it? She wondered about her mother's days and nights on her own. Had she been lonely? Betrayed? Vene made her tea and puttered upstairs. Standing in front of her mother's bedroom door, she could hear the heart monitor beeping steadily inside. She opened the door a crack and saw the night nurse reading by the lamp in the corner of the room. Her mother used to hate having to fall asleep to any amount of light. Maybe it was something you had to get used to when you were dying.

The nurse looked up from her book and nodded. The room had taken on a different aura in days of late—a sense of calm separate from the rest of the house. The doula in Vene understood the energy of a room and how not to disturb it. She took off her slippers, put her tea down, and decided to get into bed, curling into a little ball at her mother's feet, careful not to wake her. In these few moments, when she was physically close to her mother, when even their breathing patterns mimicked one another, she found the peace she longed for. And in no time at all, she fell asleep.

1946

Food for Jonathan labeled and ready

Costata di manzo al Barolo

Spaghetti Bolognese

Lasagne

Olivia had been cooking nonstop for two days—marinating and organizing the kitchen on day one, and then cooking and freezing the next. All of her dishes were Jonathan's favorite hearty meals, comfort food: spareribs cooked in red wine, spaghetti Bolognese, meat lasagna. She went so far as to make a birthday stew for eight people, ready for his next birthday. She made two batches of the other dishes and labeled the containers before placing them inside the freezer. *When I go, he will at least be well fed*, she thought, and that made her happy. Or at least less guilty.

Max entered the kitchen. "What are you doing?" he asked, confused.

There was so much she wanted to say, so much to explain. She wanted to tell him that in the end, making her decision had been easier than she had expected. It had been after the town fair when Victor received word from Italy. His father needed him, and he knew he had to go. So much had already changed, and Victor's father wanted him to take over the family business. Olivia knew they had been living under a fog of romance. Life only became real with the making of decisions and living with their consequences. She struggled to put aside blame and shame, although part of her did blame Jonathan for her insecurity, for not allowing her to be herself. And as for shame, well, that feeling nearly stopped her altogether. But for so long she'd felt shut down to the point where she no longer believed in any future with Jonathan. She had been required to be the perfect wife, a role, she told herself, that was her personal sacrifice to postwar living. And she knew it looked enviable from the outside. So many others had endured aching hardships with loved ones lost, families destroyed—why should she be spared? So she'd soldiered on with Jonathan, but it would be unfair to continue pretending she loved him in the way a woman should love her husband. She didn't, and he deserved more than that.

She wanted to tell Max that when Victor had declared his intention to leave and be a part of the rebuilding of his own country, she no longer had the strength to resist his pleas for her to join him. Here was a man willing to tell the whole world that he loved her and needed her next to him. To him, she wasn't merely a symbol of love and loyalty. Knowing that someone both needed and desired her, the way she needed and desired him, was too much to walk away from. She was in love with Victor, and her future was in Italy.

But she dared not confide in Max for fear he might talk her out of it. Max stood at attention next to the sink as if awaiting instructions. She wiped her hands on her dirty apron; they were raw from cooking and preparing. Her mouth felt dry—she'd barely eaten or drank anything all day.

"Oh, Max. It's time for me to leave. It just is. And I will miss you so."

She went to him and hugged his body. His stiff arms remained in place, but she held on nonetheless. They had never hugged before, and she felt his discomfort.

"Mrs. Winston . . ."

"No, please," she implored, "just let me say *grazie di tutto* . . . Thank you for everything, dear friend. I will always think of you when I am cooking your mother's famous stew."

She kissed him on the cheek.

Max held himself upright against the sink. She hated herself for dropping such a bombshell on him, but there was no turning back.

"I must go upstairs and pack up what I can. Victor will be here in no time, and I feel it's best to leave at night when no one is around."

She turned and raced upstairs, leaving him staring after her, in shock. The decision to leave quickly left her with no time to reconsider—and it was the only way she could go. She opened her cupboards and swept through the hangers. What would she need in Italy? What would the reinvention of her life look like? She pulled a suitcase down from the top of the closet and began filling it: blouses and slacks, a few dresses—nothing too fancy—jackets and coats, shoes for indoor and outdoor, and one or maybe two hats. She felt giddy with excitement and trepidation. *Just keep packing*, she told herself, *don't stop, don't think*. She grabbed a dressing gown and undergarments, a toiletry bag from the bathroom with essentials, and then quickly glanced in the mirror.

"You can do this," she whispered. And with a long, hard stare at herself, she took off her wedding ring and placed it in the glass dish beside the sink. "Goodbye, Jonathan."

She tried to shut the suitcase, but it wouldn't lock. She pushed and shoved the once beautifully folded clothes into untidy piles and tried again. No luck. Panic set in.

"Max!" she shouted from the top of the stairs. "Max!"

Hearing the urgency in her voice, Max came rushing up.

"Is everything all right, Mrs. Winston?"

"Max, you have to help me shut my suitcase. I can't get it to shut," she said desperately. "Here, I'll sit on it, and you can slam it shut and lock it. Ready?" She sat on top of the case. Max bent down and with a little force managed to close and lock the case.

"Thank you, Max. Thank you!" He stood and offered his hand to help her up. "Oh, Max . . . I do hope you don't hate me for what I am doing. I wish I could explain everything. Jonathan is a good man and entitled to have the right woman. But I'm not her. How could I be if I fell in love with Victor?" She crisscrossed the room, opening and shutting drawers. "I want a different life for myself, one filled with passion and food and wine. I want to live, Max, and be understood and appreciated. Victor gives me all of that. This has been the happiest month of my life, and if I don't leave now, I fear I might regret it my entire life." She stopped and looked at him beseechingly. "Please tell me that makes sense."

Before he could answer, there was the distinct sound of wheels on gravel. Victor! Olivia raced to the window. To her complete and utter horror, it wasn't Victor but Jonathan who stepped out of the car and waved up at her.

"Oh no, oh no, no no no, it can't be! Oh, dear God, no—not him. Oh, Max . . . no, no no . . ." She fell to her knees. "He won't let me go—I won't be able to go with him here! He'll make me stay . . . This wasn't supposed to happen! Why is he here? Oh God . . . Max, no!"

chapter sixteen

1996

Vene sat in a chair with a bag of yarn on her lap knitting purple cashmere into a beanie hat. It was a simple task and one that even she should have been able to complete. It wasn't exactly a usual pastime of hers, but the mindlessness of it was good enough to just pass the time. Her mother slept beside her, her frail body restless. Each time she moved, Vene watched her closely, only to see her fall back to sleep with a moan. The beeping from the heart monitor was fainter than normal, or perhaps Vene had become accustomed to it. The nurse often took a break when she was in the room, so she found herself alone with her mother. It was odd how similar this downtime was to that of a pregnant woman, who having labored for hours finally decides to have an epidural, the room going still for a while. The curtains were half drawn even though it was daytime. She had a thought to light a scented candle but somehow found the idea depressing.

She got to the end of a row and realized she'd messed up the pattern. She pulled at the yarn in frustration. "For fuck's sake," she grunted. Her mother opened one eye.

"Reading is a lot less painful," she said, her voice croaky with sleep.

"Sorry, Mom, did I wake you?"

"I'm just dozing. Dozing away."

She wondered if her mother had any realization that she slept most of the day and night. "Can I get you something?"

"Can you fix my pillows? I'd like to sit up."

Her mother's ability to speak efficiently relied on how easily she was breathing, and patience had become a necessary virtue. Vene always had so many different thoughts swirling around in her head that being forced to slow down was actually not a bad thing. She arranged the four pillows, two very firm, two goose down and soft. Her mother tried to prop herself up, but every move took a long time. Helping her mother made Vene uncomfortable. Touching her mother's legs, her skin, gave her a weird gagging sensation. She felt bad about it, but her mother was an intensely private woman, and as a child Vene had only seen her naked a few times. As an adult, never. It felt so awkward and invasive—even giving her a brief hug or lifting her leg onto a pillow felt like a warning not to go any further. So she fiddled with the pillows and sorted out the blankets, but not much more.

"How's that?" Vene asked.

"Fine, thank you."

They sat for a few moments, and Olivia started to perk up. She drank some water while Vene went back to knitting, and they settled into a comfortable silence.

"Next year you must make sure the vegetables get covered properly before the frost," Olivia said after a while. "I don't like the blankets they used this year. They nearly killed my artichokes."

"Of course, Mom. I'll tell the groundskeepers."

"They need to do it with care."

"They will."

Olivia took another sip of her water and tried to put it back on the table but fumbled. Vene quickly interceded, taking the glass and smiling at her mom gently.

"I've been reading your cookbooks, by the way. Well, not all of them, but your favorite Italian one, *Il talismano*." Vene took the book from the bedside table and held it in front of her mother.

"That's Max's mother's book."

"Max told me that he gave it to you. I never knew you enjoyed cooking so much. I nearly didn't believe him when he said those were your notes written all over it."

"Yes, well . . ." Her mother's voice trailed off.

"You seemed really happy doing it. It's weird because I don't ever remember you making one dinner growing up. Aside from penne pomodoro, that is. In London, I remember that was literally the only thing you would make."

"I couldn't bring myself to eat someone else's pomodoro."

"No one's was ever as good as yours. There are so few ingredients in a pomodoro sauce, and yet everyone's tastes different," Vene said, not wanting to make her mother feel like she was being interrogated. But she did have her attention, and that was something. She was cracking the code. "I didn't like London," she continued, playing for time.

"Really? I don't remember you not being happy."

"It was hard to fit in. The kids were mean, and it rained constantly. I remember Roxy, our dog, was my best friend. And then she got hit by that car, and the vet made us put her down."

"She had terrible breath."

"I know, but she was so cute."

"We should have put you in a British school and not the American school. Your friends kept leaving."

"Why didn't you?" Vene asked.

"Because we were always supposed to be leaving too. And then nearly ten years later, we finally did."

"Well, it was a good choice coming back to live here again.

To the estate—the grapes, your vegetable garden, the house. You must have missed it."

"It was hard to leave, yes," Olivia said.

Her mother fumbled around, putting her hands into fists and then pushing them against the mattress for leverage to lift her body up. Vene couldn't tell what she was more uncomfortable with—her position or the conversation.

"All my friends think Napa is like the land of dreams, that all the people who settle here have big visions that they are trying to make into a reality. I think of you and Dad, and how you both grew our label and make great wine. You made it so successful. It's kind of amazing."

"That wasn't my dream, Vene," she said matter-of-factly.

Vene looked at her mother, wondering how far to push it. "Then whose? I know with Dad's political work it wasn't really his."

"It was a good place to raise you. Your father was working more in the States; we'd already taken over the estate during the war. It made sense to return. People didn't always live for their dreams the way you seem to think it's inexcusable not to. People did what responsibility dictated, what was asked of them."

"I understand that, I do," she said, ignoring her mother's change of tone, "but I still don't get why you gave up cooking, though, with your vegetable garden right outside, and the harvests you loved so much."

Her mother shrugged. "When we moved to London, it was no longer necessary. Your father's position . . . it was demanding, and I had to be there for him, for you. The cook did it all—it was just easier that way. And so that became our way here as well."

"But it was so obvious you loved it. I read in so many notes how passionate you were about it. You had an entire relationship going on with your cooking."

Her mother didn't respond, so Vene pressed on. "There was even a quote from you saying your heart bled through the sauce you made." She opened the book and flipped through the pages, trying to find the quote. "It feels like you poured your whole self into these pages."

"Notes from a young woman trying to cook."

"Or trying to live . . . trying to love, it seemed."

"There was a lot to learn back then," Olivia said heavily.

"You were so young, and left alone so often. No wonder you did something to consume you. I just don't get why you stopped."

"Life doesn't always add up when you're living it," her mother said. "Sure, you can look back and put the pieces together and make sense as to why you did this or that, but not always in the moment. We weren't always happy, Vene, but we did always try."

Vene took a gamble. "Was it because of Jenny?"

"Jenny?" She smiled faintly. "Your father did almost leave me once, but it wasn't because of Jenny. Or at least, I don't think it was. Strangely, I'm actually quite fond of her."

"But if it wasn't Jenny, then what happened? You sounded heartbroken."

Her mother had a distant look on her face, clearly somewhere else. "Yes, my heart was broken once, and that was enough for me, enough for a lifetime."

"Won't you tell me what happened? Please?"

But her mother's face was like a mask. The wall was back up. There was no natural intimacy between them, and the conversation had veered into dangerous territory. Vene felt the toughness of the scar tissue surrounding her mother's heart.

"It doesn't matter anymore," Olivia said. "Now, I want to discuss my funeral because it will be very hard on your father, and it doesn't have to be. I'd like to go over the details with you because you will handle it better."

As ever, her mother managed to shut Vene down completely with a single sentence. "Sure," Vene said weakly. Something had happened to her mother, that much she knew, something bad. She wished her mother trusted her enough to tell her.

"I've spoken to Father Mark at the church in Napa, and he

agreed to do the service at the estate. I'd like to be cremated and then my ashes scattered up on the hill, by the Italian grapevines—the ones that were planted during the war when we first lived here. The ones you were named after. The view from up there is especially good, and I like the idea of going into that soil for the next harvest."

"Jesus, Mother, you really want me to cremate you and drink you later?"

"No, not you, the coroner."

"That's not funny."

"I don't want to be buried, my bones trapped in a coffin. It's time to be free."

"But Dad said he wanted you to be in a coffin, buried—eventually, I guess—next to him. He said he chose plots for the whole family, which is completely morbid, but—"

"I don't want to be in a coffin," Olivia interrupted, her voice firm.

"Did you tell him that?"

"No."

"Do you want me to?"

She didn't answer.

"What about both?" Vene suggested, thinking quickly. "You could be cremated and some of your ashes scattered and some buried in the cemetery in Napa. That way no matter what happens in the afterlife, you're covered." This was at least a little humorous, Vene thought. She knew her mother questioned God and kept that a secret from her devout father, but she didn't realize she also questioned the soul—for surely the soul could never be trapped.

"Fine," Olivia said, and then added with an edge, "after all, why stop now with your father's wishes. I've told Max not to overdo the food. Keep it simple and Italian, but you may have to watch him. He's old but he's still stubborn, and he doesn't know when to stop. I'm not interested in a big party and your father and you will be tired, so you don't have to invite the whole town. Just those who will help your father after I'm gone."

Vene felt a lump form in her throat. She swallowed a few times to keep it down. No one prepares you for these conversations, and she knew her mother needed her to abide by her wishes. She should take it as a compliment that she was the one chosen for the duty and hear her out. And the truth was, she really wanted to be there for her mom.

"I'm going to miss you, Mom," she blurted out before she couldn't.

"I've missed me for a long time already," Olivia said quietly.

The sun started dipping down, and it was getting too dark inside. Vene got up and turned on a few lights to hide her distress. Every time she felt like she was getting somewhere, her mother pulled back. She seemed to be more interested in talking about her death than her life. "Anything else?" Vene asked. There were three discreet knocks on the door.

"Max. Come in, thank you," Olivia said. "Would you please go into my top drawer over there, in the dresser? There's a parcel in there with stamps already on it. Please mail it." Max had to move his hand deep into the drawer to find the parcel. It was thick, as if it contained many letters. "I don't trust the nurses to mail it, so I want you to do it. Please just make sure you do it tomorrow. Take it directly to the post office. It's heavy so please bring extra money, just in case I didn't put enough stamps on it."

"Of course, Mrs. Winston. I'll go tomorrow."

"Good. Thank you." She closed her eyes, making it clear she was done talking. She started dozing again, her jaw slack, her mouth open, a slight rattle in her chest. Vene leaned over and looked at the name on the parcel in Max's hands, but there was only a PO box. The parcel was sealed with her mother's trademark gold seal on the back, the kind that requires you to heat the wax first to make it stick. So old-fashioned, she thought. Only her mother still sealed envelopes like this.

"Who lives in Italy?" she asked Max.

Max glanced at Olivia.

"Obviously she doesn't care that I know she's sending a parcel to Italy otherwise she wouldn't have given it to you in front of me. Who is it addressed to?" Vene tried reading Max's face, but he gave away nothing.

"It's a vineyard, I believe. In Tuscany," he said.

"Which vineyard? Friends of hers? Is it to do with business?"

"I don't know, Vene. It's not my parcel."

"Well, it's obviously important to her. Do you know what's in it? Paperwork of some sort? How often does she write to that address?"

Max didn't respond.

"Max?"

"Not that often. I don't keep a record."

"I can go to the post office later today if you want?"

"No. That's okay. I'll go myself," he replied, leaving the room abruptly. Vene stayed, watching her mother rest. What had she meant about her heart being broken? Max was definitely being discreet about something. "Mom? You still awake?" she whispered. She picked up the *Il talismano* cookbook. The person who had written these notes was buried deep inside of her mother, and she seemed determined to keep it that way. She'd been prepared to let Vene in a little, but Vene needed more. But how?

Vene continued to read, flipping more pages impatiently. Then on a whim, she snapped the book shut and opened the drawer her mother had kept her package in, rummaging around right at the back. Suddenly she felt a click, and a shallow tray of a shelf sprang out with what looked like a letter on top. It had creases on it from having been read and reread, folded and refolded. Vene glanced at her mother, but she didn't stir. She pulled out the paper and sat on the edge of the bed.

December 10th, 1946

Dear Jonathan,

Forgive me my sins. I cannot go on. My heart has been stripped bare. It is not your fault; it is solely mine. I have broken into tiny pieces and can never be put back together again. I need to end the pain that torments me every hour of every day. I have failed you as a wife. I pray for your happiness. This will be a blessing for you too in time. I am so sorry. This baby cannot be. I am too empty now, and love cannot grow inside of me. I fear too much and realize now I would have been a terrible mother. This is meant to be. I am sorry—goodbye.

Olivia

As Vene read, her horror grew. Pain seeped off the page like an open wound. She read it again. She could scarcely believe it, but at the same time she knew it must be true. Her mother had tried to kill herself.

1946

Max's easy eating dinner menu

Palline di formaggio e salsiccia

Spaghetti pesto

Carne di maiale con erbe

It had been the first day in a long time that Olivia had stayed out of the kitchen entirely. With Jonathan home, the spell had been broken and all the magic that cooking brought her disappeared. She had managed to put all of her clothes back in time before he'd knocked on their bedroom door, and she'd covered her panic as he entered. After one month away, this was supposed to be a reunion. She knew Jonathan had missed her and was longing to see her. Here was a man who carried his wife's photo in his wallet. But upon entering the room, instead of sweeping her up in his arms and expressing his love for her, he remained utterly true to character.

"Hello, darling," he said, giving her a brief hug and kiss, "it's so good to see you."

For once his formality suited her. And if her body was shaking, he was too weary and tired to notice—more anxious to shower off the long journey than linger. Olivia was desperate to gather herself.

One week later, the heaviness remained between them. Olivia wondered if he too had changed, fallen out of love, and wanted a way out of their marriage. From the moment he'd arrived home, he was either completely wrapped up in Washington phone calls, locked away in his study; or focused on the estate, studying the breakdown of the harvest, analyzing sales and the plans ahead. He seemed to be obsessed with his work more than ever. One night, they were to have dinner with Victor to go over all the details of the business. Max did all the cooking, and Olivia hid upstairs for as long as she could, too nervous to come down.

Victor had arrived twenty minutes early, and she was sure he and Jonathan were having a drink in the study. Her mind raced around for some stabilizing thought or image. She hadn't been able to explain herself to Victor since Jonathan's arrival and was desperate for some time alone with him. Their escape plan had been just that, a quick way out, and now she needed a new plan. It wasn't easy to organize, and it was expensive. Heathrow Airport near London, England, had recently opened for civilian use, and their plan was to fly there and then take a boat to France, after which they'd make their way to Italy. It was a complicated journey and tickets were difficult to get without alerting someone she knew, so she was going to have to rely on Victor for everything. Guilt and loyalty pulled her one way, but her heart was stronger. Still, she was afraid and needed more time. She searched her velvet jewelry box and found a gold pendant with a small pearl in the middle, her birthstone. It was the first piece of jewelry she had bought herself and a reminder of the woman she dreamed of becoming one day. A woman who was excited by life, and who believed in herself. She clasped the chain around her neck like a touchstone.

Max rang the dinner bell, and she felt almost physically sick at the idea of seeing Victor.

"Coming," she called. She had put on a beautiful burgundy swing dress, cinched at the waist with three-quarter sleeves and a wonderful flare at the bottom—dressing for the occasion. What kind of occasion, however, was the question. She made her way out of her room and down the main staircase. Jonathan and Victor were coming out of the study with their drinks as she reached the bottom step. They both looked up at her.

"You look lovely tonight, darling," Jonathan said admiringly.

"Yes, you do," Victor said softly.

Olivia held on to the banister and said nothing, letting them pass first. All she could do was smile back and follow from behind. Max had laid the long mahogany table beautifully, with three seats together at one end. Olivia was at the head and Jonathan and Victor on either side. Max was trying not to catch her eye as she sat down. She felt as if he'd been avoiding her all week. He placed the appetizers down on the table as they sat, then discreetly left the room. She wanted Max to see her pain and confusion but understood how awkward and conflicted he must feel watching her perform her duty.

Victor decanted some red wine and then poured Olivia a glass of Puligny-Montrachet, her favorite white. She smiled.

"Pour me a glass too, Victor, if you will. I'd prefer to start with white," Jonathan said. Victor handed him one and he took a quick sip. "Fresh and crisp, yet full-bodied. Very nice," he commented. "I made it a point in Paris to try some incredible European wines—really impressive quality over there."

"It's been my hope to make equally impressive wine in Napa," Victor replied.

"Yes, yes, I agree. There was some talk over there about our small wine region. Dare I say I think a few of their winemakers are more than intrigued. The vintner group is successfully putting Napa on the map. Inglenook, Louis, the Mondavis, the whole lot of them. It's good for us. Good for you."

"They are interested in how we are blending. Everything grows very well here. Back in Italy, I was already experimenting with different varietals. I used the French oak barrels for storing and imported some of their vines as well. I was trying to create a more refined, complex Italian wine. Most winemakers in Tuscany were only making Chianti from old recipes using large Slovenian barrels. I blended from afar as well as locally and stopped using white grapes altogether. There were a few men doing the same, Rocchetta and a few others. But most were still skeptical."

"Yes, I have heard of him," Jonathan said. "Well, you have my support to do it all here—take the reins. In fact, that is why I asked you for dinner tonight. I wanted to discuss your future here."

Victor glanced quickly at Olivia, who looked down at her food.

"My future here?"

"Yes, indeed. My wife and I will be leaving the estate in less than two weeks for London," Jonathan said matter-of-factly.

Olivia looked up. "What?"

"Yes, darling, I got the call this afternoon and thought I'd surprise you at dinner with the good news."

"What news?"

"I know how you've been feeling cut off living here and not very happy."

"No, I haven't. Or not for a very long time," Olivia replied defensively. "What are you talking about, Jonathan?"

"Darling, President Truman himself called and asked me to be his ambassador to the UK. There were rumors at the Paris Peace Conference, but nothing was guaranteed. Lewis Douglas was set to take over from Harriman, so I'm not sure how long the post will be for, but my lord, it's incredible news, isn't it?" Jonathan looked at Olivia, excitement and pride in his wide smile.

Olivia gulped at her wine. She looked over at Victor, who was staring back at her.

"I . . . I . . . I don't know what to say," Olivia stammered.

Jonathan reached over and touched her hand. "I know, darling, I know, it's incredible. All of my hard work, those days and nights away, and Truman is finally rewarding me publicly. I can't say that's all I wanted, but hey, that's all I wanted! I've been busting to tell you," he said, laughing.

Olivia found it hard to breathe. Her world was spinning out of control.

"Max!" Jonathan shouted. "Max!"

Max came into the room. "Yes, Mr. Winston?"

"Champagne, Max. Please bring in a bottle of champagne. We are toasting tonight."

"Jonathan, this is so sudden," Olivia said. "A very big change for you."

"For us, sweetheart. *We* will be leaving. I will tell Max, and the staff will have to work together to arrange everything for you. Whatever we can't bring now can be sent later."

"To London?"

"Yes, to London. Now, Victor, this brings me to you."

Max entered with the champagne and Victor stood, taking the bottle from Max. "Allow me, Max," he said calmly, expertly popping the cork and pouring out three glasses. "Congratulations, Mr. Winston—*Ambassador*," Victor said, clinking his glass to Jonathan's.

Olivia froze. Less than two weeks? Her hands began to shake. She folded them in her lap.

"Thank you, Victor. So, the estate. I trust you are happy here? I would be indebted to you if you were to stay on and run the entire operation. I can offer you some stake in the vineyard to sweeten the deal, and I would rely fully upon your expertise to make all viniculture decisions as winemaker. You would have my full backing. I have heard from Louis Martini and the Mondavis how exceptional you are."

"Oh my," Olivia said quietly. "I don't feel very well."

"Perhaps some water." Victor took her glass, looking at her straight in the eye. She looked back at him pleadingly, desperate for an answer to this terrible mess.

"Thank you," she said, taking a sip.

"I appreciate the offer and your trust, especially after such a short time here at the estate." Victor turned to Jonathan. "Louis is the reason I am in Napa, and I have been an admirer of his for a long time. However, with the war over, and reparations being made, my heart—although it has been here creating wonderful things"—again he looked at Olivia—"belongs back in Italy.

My future is there. I'm just not sure how long I could commit to you."

"The groundskeepers tell me you have planted root stalks from Italy. Surely you'd like to see them harvested?"

"Jonathan, this is all so unexpected," Olivia blurted out. "I can't possibly leave in less than two weeks. You should go and I will organize the house, the estate. It makes sense for you to leave first. There's so much to do here, and you will be so busy over there."

"No, don't be silly. Besides, I can't have the wife of the ambassador traveling abroad by herself. It simply wouldn't look right," he insisted, smiling firmly.

Olivia looked from Jonathan to Victor. Jonathan was lost in his own accomplishments, and Victor was searching her face for an answer.

Max reentered with spaghetti pesto. As he put the food in front of her, Olivia got up, nauseous at the smell. She excused herself, but before she reached the door, the room began to spin. She grabbed the back of the nearest chair, but it was no use. She fainted, collapsing onto the floor. Both men instinctively rushed over. Victor crouched down first and held her head and then her hand. Jonathan shook her gently by the shoulders until her eyes finally opened. Incoherent, she turned to them, reaching her other hand up, and said, "Oh, Victor." For a moment, Jonathan stared at Victor. Then he took his wife's hand from him and turned his back on his vintner, marking his presence. Out of respect, and overcome by emotion, Oliva saw Victor back away.

chapter seventeen

1996

It wasn't a particularly good morning. The fog hadn't yet lifted from the valley floor, and the air was cool, going on cold. The house was never able to warm up evenly; some rooms were like a sauna while others remained chilly, and the hallways were always crisp. Vene was upstairs having a shower. Her room, in particular, was always freezing. The hotter her parents made their room, the colder hers became. She'd had a bulb installed, recessed into the ceiling of her shower, that turned bright red and radiated the most incredible heat so when she took showers her whole body warmed up. She stood there soaking the heat into her bones. So much had been revealed in the past few days, and yet there was nothing she could do. There was never a good opportunity to speak to her mother about the letter, and even if there had been, what good would it do now? Grief was exhausting and her mother hadn't even died yet. It had been a few weeks since Vene arrived back home, and it could still be weeks more. As each day passed, so too did her energy.

She had just finished her shower when she heard the doorbell. She went to the window and saw the very familiar Mustang in the driveway. Fiona Patterson, her childhood best friend—her bright peach tracksuit clashing with her wild red hair—was getting out of her car. Vene quickly changed and ran downstairs as eagerly as she might have forty years ago.

Max opened the door, and Fiona wrapped her arms around his semi-frail body in a huge hug. Vene had to laugh at her way of dispelling formality. Fiona had always been Max's favorite out of her friends, and she could tell he was enjoying the squeeze.

"Fi Fi!" Vene exclaimed, pushing her way in for a group hug.

"Venerdi! Ciao, sister!" Fiona said in her booming voice. "How the hell are you?" she asked, twirling her around.

"Oh my God, I swear you are the only one who ever calls me that. I haven't heard my full name since I was about five."

"Born on a Friday! Or conceived on a Friday, what was it? I never could remember. You can never make a new old friend, sister. Ever. That's what keeps me special."

"And today we are the youngest we're ever going to be."

"Hear, hear!" Fiona said. "That's a good one, I like it! Come on, let's drink."

"It's ten a.m."

"And your point is?"

As always, Max looked to be enjoying their banter.

"We need to get stuff done first," Vene pointed out.

"I am not going to see the Dracula place without alcohol in me."

"How about a mimosa?" Vene suggested.

"Perfecto."

"Allow me," Max said, withdrawing with a smile. Fiona took Vene's arm and pulled her to sit underneath the curving swirl of the main staircase, an old hideout of theirs that had almost become a ritual of sorts.

"Thanks for coming. I really didn't want to do this on my own," Vene said.

"I get it."

Vene looked at her friend. They'd been close for forty years, and there was nothing Fiona didn't know about her.

"I had my first kiss sitting right here," Fiona said. "Oh my God . . . do you remember Teddy Dritikin? He swirled his tongue around my mouth like he was trying to literally touch each and every tooth in there. Totally grossed me out." She laughed.

"Then you made me kiss Walter Bingham, which was so unfair," Vene remembered.

"I heard he only liked boys after that."

"Forever traumatized by a twelve-year-old female tongue."

"If your parents had known what we got up to, I'm not so sure you would have made it to thirteen."

"The lying started young for sure." Vene paused. "I liked it here. I used to pretend no one could see me, that this was my invisible spot. But then I seemed to remain invisible regardless of being here."

"This was also your favorite silent treatment spot," Fiona said.

"What is that supposed to mean?"

"When you were giving someone the silent treatment, you used to sit under here and stew away."

"That is so not true," Vene protested.

"So is."

"I don't give people the silent treatment when I'm mad."

"Maybe not anymore, but you were the queen of it when we were younger," Fiona replied.

"Well, I learned from the expert."

"At least you weren't sent to shrinks to be analyzed your whole life."

Vene grabbed Fiona's hand. "Doesn't matter how long it's been since I've seen you, it's always the same."

"Friends till the end, sista."

"Friends till the end."

Max appeared in front of them with a tray of mimosas.

"Come on." Fiona hoisted herself up and put out her hand to do the same for Vene. "Let's get this over with."

They both took a glass and downed it in one. Fiona burped, and they laughed as they headed through the front door.

"Ciao, Max. We'll be back for more!" Fiona shouted after them.

Tulocay Cemetery was a funeral home in Napa that had been operating since the 1800s. Olivia had specifically wanted Vene to arrange everything through them, as she and Jonathan personally knew the family who ran it and they knew Father Mark. It was apparently the "right" thing to do, organizing these things ahead of time when grief wasn't yet overwhelming. Nevertheless, Vene had felt very strange making an appointment while her mother was still alive.

The Mustang pulled up to the front, Seal's "Don't Cry" blaring through the door speakers.

"I dreamt of this place many times," Fiona said, staring at the graves.

"You're weird."

"It was a fantasy, where I would bury Freddie. I got off on it."

"Freddie?"

"Husband number three, remember?"

"Ah, Freddie. Short and sweet."

"He was neither short nor sweet," Fiona pointed out.

"Tall and tart?"

"Something like that. Lasted only six months, but he still managed to leave a bad taste in my mouth, that's for sure."

"Many men have left a bad taste in your mouth," Vene replied.

"Yeah, yeah."

"Just sayin'."

They walked into the funeral parlor to be greeted by Stephanie, the funeral director, who was wearing a skirt down to her calves with a huge animal print on it. Fiona and Vene did a double take. She had to be the most old-fashioned thirtysomething woman they had ever seen. The entrance of the building was warm and decorated like someone's living room—no doubt to make the bereaved comfortable, and it clearly worked. It was a long-standing family-run business that did a good job of creating an atmosphere like you'd been invited there for nothing more than a cup of tea.

"Hello, I'm Stephanie," she said, shaking their hands. "I'm so sorry to meet you under these difficult circumstances." She followed everything she said with a reassuring nod.

"Yes," Vene answered.

"Difficult," Fiona repeated.

"I understand Father Mark will be doing the service, both here and at the estate. And that you would like an in-ground burial with a coffin here as well as a service with a scattering of ashes at the estate."

"My mother wasted no time in telling you the specifics. That's good."

"She's a very . . . forthright lady," Stephanie said. "It's not too typical to speak with someone in so much detail about their burial, but I find it's much better for the family to have that clarity."

"Wouldn't want to leave anything up to me, that's for sure," Vene replied, the hurt evident in her voice.

"Yes, well," Stephanie continued, moving sweetly over the sarcasm, "would you care for something to drink before we choose the coffin? Coffee, tea, water?"

"Or something a bit stronger, perhaps," Fiona said. "Grieving and all . . ."

Stephanie checked her watch but took her cue, leaving to get the wine after Fiona just smiled back. This was Napa, after all.

Fiona turned to Vene. "Your mom's been controlling your whole life, right? Get over it. It's really time to get over it."

"I still feel like I'm ten years old wanting her approval."

"She hated your taste in clothes, makeup, hair, men . . . but she didn't hate you."

"She actually still talks to me about boring Robert, for fuck's sake!"

"Robert's a loser. Anyone friends with *my* first ex is seriously a questionable person. You got it right with Tony. Fuck your mother—she's just jealous. I mean, I love her, even though she scares the living shit outta me, but something in her could never be happy for you, and that's on her, not you."

"You tried to get it right. With your parents, I mean," Vene said.

"Not really. You know we were never really close. My dad drank so much, and my mom, well, as ever, she's the optimist with her stash of cash and revolving door of suitors after my dad died. Having a trust fund allowed me to not feel desperate with men, but it made for bad choices and no sense of who the hell I am."

"Really?"

"So says my therapist," Fiona replied.

"I don't want the money."

"So says the girl about to inherit a lot of it! Honestly, Vene, what did you expect was going to happen when you got back?

"I didn't expect to feel sorry for her."

"Yeah, well, cancer sucks."

"No, not that. I mean it's awful, but I'm getting my head around that, I guess. It's more about all the things I've been reading in her cookbooks—they read like a diary," Vene explained. "You'd be properly shocked."

"Like what?"

"She used to be such a free-sounding spirit—seriously full of passion. Spontaneous, even."

"Like you."

"I think she and I would have been good friends back then."

"Wow."

"There was definitely a desire for more. A restlessness. It's so weird, Fi . . . you should read some of the comments about lust and heat and cooking things that didn't seem to be in the kitchen!"

"No, thank you."

"Honestly, what she was really up to, who knows. Her heart was bursting, but for whom, I actually don't know. And then . . ."

"What?"

"Tragedy."

"Really? What do you mean?" Fiona asked. "What tragedy?"

Vene suddenly thought better of telling Fi about the letter. "I don't know—all sorts. But what I'm sure of is that the woman who wrote in that book never presented herself to me. I literally feel like I've never seen the real her. Like she was left behind at some point."

"Maybe it was made up—a make-believe life she was writing about—a wanderlust?"

"No—it feels too real. It's as if she was two different people, a before and an after. As if from the moment I was born, the controlling, hard-nosed, dutiful version was born too."

"Which version did your dad get?"

"I don't know. A cold one."

"Well then, let's go and pick out a steel coffin."

Vene knew Fiona was trying to make light, but knowing her mother's intense sadness now highlighted her mother's coldness differently. "It's all such a waste. And I'm trying to make sense out of why. And I can't. I think my dad may have had an affair with Jenny, which would explain a lot of their . . . I don't know, rigidness between them. Why their love never felt easy to me."

"I remember Jenny. Do you really think she'd be around in the open as often as she was if they were having an affair? That doesn't add up to me. Your dad just doesn't seem the type."

"I know. But when you read her cookbooks, it makes sense. There's escapism written all over them. But it's not just about Jenny. My mom made it a huge point to give Max a parcel in front of me to send to a PO box in Italy. She's apparently sent stuff there before."

"That's wild. Who lives there?"

"I don't know yet—but I'll find out."

Vene looked out the window at all the gravestones. "I just want to understand who she really is. And every time we talk now, which is never for long, she doesn't have the energy for long conversations anymore; it's more of the same, and there's so much regret on my part for not being able to sit with her comfortably and accept the mother that she was. That she is."

"You're also grieving for the mother you never had."

Vene started to cry. The tears just poured out of her, and for once and she didn't hold them back. Fiona wrapped her arms around her and rocked her gently.

"Why do I care so much?" Vene whispered.

"Cuz she's your mom."

"I wish I could just let it go—everyone tells me to let it go, but I don't want to. I'm so fucking mad at her, it's unbelievable. I'm able to walk away and be sure of myself with everything and everyone in my life, except her."

Fiona wiped the tears and held her friend's face. "She loves you, Venerdi," she said fiercely. "I can see that so clearly. I swear to God. She loves you the best way she knows how."

"I want to give her some sort of peace. In life and with me . . . but it's so hard to know what to do and what to say."

"Maybe it's really simple. Maybe what you see is what you get? Sounds like you are overthinking it."

"Maybe."

"Steel coffin?" Fiona asked.

"Steel coffin," Vene agreed, but even as she said it, she realized she no longer believed it.

1946

Mama's chicken soup, and something sweet for energy

Zuppa di pollo, pane

Mele al forno con limone e zucchero

The doctor's office was a small building in St. Helena connected to an even smaller local hospital where Olivia usually went for her female checkups. Usually when one of them was ill, the doctor came to the estate, but this was an emergency and no sooner had Jonathan gotten Olivia through the door than she collapsed again. They had been running tests all night, with Jonathan dozing uncomfortably in the waiting room outside, and now Olivia lay in bed in her examination gown while a nurse took her vital signs.

"Where did you go?" Olivia asked, feeling frightened, as Jonathan walked into the room.

"I was speaking to the doctor outside. He confirmed everything I already knew."

"Knew?"

"That you are completely fine and that this is all anxiety."

"Jonathan, what are you talking about? What did he say? Why am I fainting?"

He took a minute before he could actually form the words. "We're pregnant."

"What?!"

"Well, you're pregnant, I'm just a small part of it. Darling, we're going to have a baby," he said, looking and sounding overjoyed.

Olivia thought she might faint again. Dear God. The near constant nausea, the feeling so unwell—of course, it all made sense. All except for the "how."

"I told you nothing was wrong with you. I said you would eventually get the job done." Jonathan was beaming at her, looking right through her, she couldn't help but think, into his legacy. *There's nothing wrong with me*, she thought wildly, then almost simultaneously she realized what that meant. That it was Jonathan who couldn't have children, not her. She tried to find his eyes, but she could see he was already living in their future.

"How pregnant?"

"Had to have been my last trip back, so more than a month—probably several," Jonathan said happily. "The doctor wants to know the last time you menstruated. Things like that. You can talk to him about all of your feminine details." He went to her bedside. "You're going to have to be very careful. After all, this is everything you ever wanted. And now with my job, London, well, this is all very good news indeed."

Sheer terror gripped her body at the trap she was in. A baby? She was having Victor's baby? She must get to him. She had to see him immediately.

She struggled off the examination table.

"I need to get dressed. Could everyone please leave the room? We need to go."

"Mrs. Winston," the nurse said, "if you'll just wait a few more minutes, the doctor will want to see you and go over all the things you'll need to know for the pregnancy."

"Yes, darling, we need to wait for the doctor," Jonathan echoed.

"No, I need to get home. Please, Jonathan."

"I understand you must be shocked, you poor thing. All this time you thought something was wrong with you, but nothing is wrong. In fact, everything is right. Everything is perfect. Why don't you get dressed and I will go and get the doctor, all right? You look very pale." He touched her arm and she recoiled. Jonathan removed his hand as though he'd been stung.

"I'm fine. Please. Nurse, please go with my husband and help him find the doctor," Olivia said as calmly as she could. She was desperate to be left alone, if only for a minute.

"Of course, ma'am." As soon as the nurse and Jonathan had gone, Olivia manically started putting on her clothes. A baby . . . Victor's baby. It had to be, and that was reason enough to confess her sins to Jonathan and leave him once and for all.

They rode home in silence, Olivia suddenly euphoric, the doctor's words resonating in her ears: *Congratulations. You must be so relieved. Take great care of yourself in the coming months.* It was the ultimate sign she needed to finally leave. Jonathan stared silently through the car window while Olivia's thoughts raced on through every fractured memory of the past weeks. She knew one thing for certain, that her love for Victor was real and the most honest feeling she had. And now his baby was growing inside of her—a tangible proof of that love.

The driver pulled up to the house, and Max greeted them immediately. The remainder of the house staff stood inside the doorway as a show of respect at their arrival, no doubt having assumed something was seriously wrong. After all, Olivia had fainted in front of everyone only the evening before.

"I need to make a few calls to Washington right now," Jonathan said as they entered. "You should go upstairs and have a bath. I'll see you for dinner." He kissed her on her cheek, then walked into his study and shut the door.

Olivia turned to Max. "Where is Victor?" she said bluntly.

"I'm not sure, Mrs. Winston."

"I need to see him. When did you see him last? Was he here at the house or up at the vines?"

"I haven't seen him all day. Not at the vineyard either."

"I need to talk to him, Max. I'm taking the car and going to his cottage. If Mr. Winston tries looking for me, tell him I'm in the bath."

"But . . ."

"Just do it, Max. Please," she said.

"Should you be driving yourself?" Max asked. "I could have the driver take you?"

"No, I want to go on my own." She looked pleadingly at Max, the keeper of all her secrets, the only person who knew what she was going through. She trusted him more than anyone else in her life. "Thank you." She touched his arm, then raced through the front door to the Rolls-Royce, driving with an urgency she'd never felt before. Her life was about to change, finally and forever.

It had been dusk when they arrived home, and now as darkness fell the evening haze thickened into fog. Olivia was an inexperienced driver. The dirt road around the property was narrow and steep, with no lights to guide her. She skidded on a few turns, the car's wheels spinning, kicking up dust and destroying the shrubs lining the pathway to the cottage. She knew every turn, every bend in that drive. How many nights had she found solace there? She got out of the car and ran to the door, wildly excited. She had made her decision and couldn't wait another second to tell him.

Inside the lights were off, save for a yellow bulb glowing in an old lantern by the door. She knocked furiously, and then banged on the thick wood. "Victor, Victor!" She ran to the side window and peered in, but she couldn't see anything. "Victor!" she shouted again, banging on the windowpane. "Victor! I'm here!" Still she heard nothing and she stepped back, a little dismayed. She noticed that the estate car Victor normally used was parked in the driveway. He couldn't be far. She ran to the back of the cottage and then up onto the hill behind, yelling his name over and over and over again. It was cold outside, and a sudden chill ran through her body. Where was he?

She ran round the back of the cottage and found the spare key under its stone. She snapped on the lights and hurried from room to room, feeling increasingly desperate. The kitchen table was bare, a single chair pushed up to it. Victor's bed was made, and the pillow with a yellow bird she'd embroidered for him was perched against the headboard. She looked around for some sign of life, scattered belongings, books, anything . . . but there was nothing except the cold slap of reality. He was gone.

chapter eighteen

1996

Lloyd Matthews had been the Winston Family winemaker for the past ten years. He was the fifth winemaker they had employed since the war, each taking on their own decade of challenges and accomplishments. Jonathan had fully relied on Lloyd to make all the decisions about the vineyard, and the new majority shareholders were equally impressed with his expertise. Meetings with Lloyd were always outside on the grounds, up on the hill next to the vines.

Jonathan needed the fresh air and encouraged Vene to come with him to the meeting. Together they walked slowly up onto the back of the property, high on the hill, where the Italian grapes had been planted so many years ago. He now used an old walking stick made out of oak. He had a different one for indoors, but this one was more robust looking. He was still a fast walker with an impossibly long stride. She remembered nearly having to run to keep up with his pace, or at least take small, quick steps alongside him to stay in sync.

On top of the hill, they could see much of the valley below. It was a view neither of them ever tired of. Lloyd was already at the Italian grapes, inspecting the vines after the recent harvest.

"These vines have always been my favorite at the estate. These grapes make our cab what it is. The valley is always jealous of these ones," Lloyd explained. "Wish we had planted more."

"Why didn't we?" Vene asked.

"The vines were grafted from Italian roots during the war. A few different varietals, Bordeaux with sangiovese grapes. Suppose that's all that was brought over."

"After the war," Jonathan noted.

"Sorry?" Lloyd said.

"It was just after the war that he was here," Jonathan said emphatically.

"Yes, of course, not during, but after the war."

"Why did we plant Italian grapes?" Vene asked.

"It was a brilliant idea, albeit not a popular one at the time," Lloyd explained. "Victor Viandanti was the estate's winemaker, and he was way ahead of the game, a true force. Shame he only stayed for a short while. I give him credit for how successful your namesake reserve has become. Venerdi . . . a bottle from the 1947 vintage, arguably one of our finest years, recently sold for over eight hundred dollars. The fruit was so well preserved and had persistence on the finish that rivaled even Inglenook's at the time. All Viandanti's vision."

"I guess not many people can say they are named after a wine," Vene remarked.

"Your mother came up with the name. She loved it up here. She decided you were going to be as beautiful as this hilltop," Jonathan said tenderly. Unlike her mother, her father's love for her was always so close to the surface.

"And Mr. Viandanti—why did he leave? Which label did he go to next?" Vene asked.

"He went back to Tuscany," Lloyd said.

"Tuscany? Why Tuscany?"

"His family has their own remarkable vineyard, thousands of acres. I met him there once. He showed me a thing or two, and boy, was he an artist with wine. Unique. He seemed to have had a love affair with anything to do with it. The vines, the blending, this place too, I'm sure," Lloyd said, and Vene was suddenly aware of a pinprick of curiosity. "The Viandantis were a part of the first winemakers who invented the complex Tuscan wines we have today," he continued blithely. "Super Tuscan wine, it's called."

"Of course, the Super Tuscans," Vene murmured.

"He played around with adding different varietals to the grapes in Chianti, and storing them in French oak barrels instead of steel casks. It was completely unheard of at the time, and also forbidden by the Italian authorities governing wine distribution. His vision was validated in the seventies, although he never got any acknowledgment for it. I've told your father many times that we've been lucky—the estate was touched by the hand of a genius."

"Why did he leave here?" Vene asked.

"He had his own life to get back to," Jonathan said.

"It was a long time ago, 1947," Lloyd added.

"No. It was December 1946," her father corrected, but Vene didn't miss the slight edge that had crept into his voice.

"Yes, sorry, end of '46. And as the story goes, it was a sudden departure. No one in the valley seemed to know much about his time here. Not sure he ever came back, even to visit."

"Not as far as I know," Jonathan said.

"But you knew him well, Dad?" Vene probed.

"He understood wine," her father said brusquely.

Lloyd added, "The Viandanti estate is now run by Victor's sister, Anna. It's not the same. She's made some strange decisions not in keeping with his level of excellence."

"Is he dead?" Vene asked.

"No. He's pretty old now and a bit of a recluse, never married, no kids. Very different from the man I met years back. Big mistake, though, to pass the estate onto his family. The last vintage produced under his name was actually a reserve. Come to think of it, it was called Venerdi as well. I'd say that was a nod to the Winston Estate."

"That's so interesting, right, Dad?"

"Let's get on with the meeting, shall we?" Jonathan snapped. "I haven't got all day."

1946

Menu—back to the basics

Minestrone

Penne pomodoro

Crostata al cioccolato

Max had been cooking since early morning. Alone. Olivia had not only stopped eating much but had stopped cooking altogether; she barely stepped into the kitchen. In the few days since Victor's abrupt departure, she walked around in a daze of loneliness and depression, all the light gone from her eyes. If ever a person could appear on the outside exactly how they were feeling on the inside, this was it. She was the picture of heartbreak.

Max made sure he prepared all of the recipes his mother had taught him to cook that were good for pregnancy: lots of vegetables, plenty of protein, and chocolate as a treat. But no matter how much time he spent preparing her favorites, she pushed the food around her plate. He tried his specialty comfort food, pasta pomodoro—his family's recipe that she had mastered. It had been the meal she cooked that first impressed Victor and Max was sure she would eat it, but she only complained of being too nauseous. It was as if she hated eating in front of Jonathan, and he was constantly worried she wasn't feeding the baby enough nutrients. He had taken a close interest in her health since the pregnancy, and it annoyed her. All eyes were on her, she knew, to make sure she was ready and healthy for the big move. They were supposed to be traveling by the end of the week, and the journey would be a long one. TWA airline, Jonathan excitedly told her, boasted the best air-pressurized cabins with the most comfort. They were using the latest Boeing Stratoliner aircraft, and he'd booked the finest seats money could buy. Foreign travel was on the rise again, and there were diplomatic conferences scheduled for Paris, Geneva, and London in the following few months. He wanted Olivia to be able to settle into their new residence as soon as possible so that he could leave her without any guilt—or at least that's what she privately believed.

Olivia thought constantly about arguing her case to remain in Napa. Jonathan's challenging schedule and the risk of too much travel during her pregnancy were convincing excuses, but she also feared remaining would make her feel even worse. Every empty corner of the estate was a reminder of Victor's absence. He'd left her and their love—her life forever suspended. She was tormented, enraged. How could he abandon her like that? Make the decision for them both just like that! And now there was a baby, his baby, and he was gone, leaving her more desperate than ever. It was terrible to admit, but if something had happened to the baby early on, it would almost have come as a relief. The guilt over her secret would be released, and she wouldn't owe Jonathan anything. She could be brave and leave him and show Victor he was right; they could start their life over together in Italy. But each day as the baby grew, so too did the weight of her sins and sacrifices, and somehow she just knew she'd be trapped forever. The baby would have to come first. She would never tell Jonathan the truth, and her baby would never know their remarkable father.

Victor's abrupt departure also meant that Jonathan had to replace him immediately, and interviews for a new winemaker were underway. Each candidate commented on Victor's innovative style and the varietals he planted from Europe. Jonathan was less interested in the wine and more focused on whom he could entrust the financial running of the vineyard, as he predicted that he and Olivia would be away for several years at minimum. Her life was being dictated, and she felt as though she'd lost all control over her future. Only weeks before, she'd been preparing to let go of everything, Jonathan included. Today, she sat motionless, without a voice, without hope. The only thing she'd insisted on was the naming of the first harvest with the grapes Victor had planted from Italy: Venerdi. It had been a Friday when Victor vanished, and the last day she would ever feel truly complete.

One evening she was upstairs in her room as the chambermaids were packing her belongings. Three women were carefully wrapping shoes and clothes, jewelry and hats into three large trunks. It was cold in Europe, and there was an entire case of furs she had almost never worn in Napa. Life in London was definitely statelier than Northern California, and given her expanding waistline, she would have to have a seamstress make her several new dresses upon arrival. She'd become accustomed to wearing informal, carefree country clothes, but a diplomat's wife was supposed to keep up appearances, and a few London designers had already been notified of her imminent arrival. For some women, this would have been an exciting prospect, but Olivia saw the clothes as a uniform and dreaded it.

Overseeing the packing, she suddenly spotted her *Il talismano* cookbook on top of her bed. Max must have put it there, she thought. She sat down by the window and flipped through the book, slowly reading the symbols scrawled in its pages, her notes and confessions. Perhaps Max cooking her pasta pomodoro today was an attempt to remind her of the first lessons he'd given her and the spirit she'd discovered in herself. She turned to the recipe:

Max infused the oil with lots of basil beforehand. Make sure to scrunch up the basil in your hand to release the natural oils of the plant before adding to olive oil. Makes your hand smell delicious too. A passed-down secret used to inspire. It worked!

She knew Max's intentions had been to reignite her spark. Instead, seeing the book terrified her. The prospect of living this lie, this life, without any hope made her feel like she was drowning in sadness—not to mention the stress she was causing her unborn child. She stared out the window. It was a gray day, heavy with clouds. The last time she had packed her bags, she'd been looking forward to a sunny future in Italy. She'd had a giddy excitement along with her conviction that she was right to follow her heart. And now her heart ached so much she had to press her hands to her chest. There was only one thing left to do, a single act of honesty left to her.

She told the chambermaids to leave her. She went into her drawer and took out some paper and a pen.

Dear Jonathan . . . she began.

When she had finished, she blew dry the ink on the page slowly and methodically. She placed the letter on their bed and walked into the bathroom, turned the bath on, and locked the door behind her.

Max was in the kitchen reducing a Marsala sauce for their chicken dish that night. As he stirred gently, a drop of water fell into his saucepan. And then another. He looked up. For a moment he stood frozen, then he dropped his spoon and took the stairs, two steps at a time, pushing open the master bedroom door without hesitation. Water was flowing into the room from underneath the bathroom door. He tried the handle, then banged with his fist. "Mrs. Winston! Mrs. Winston!" he shouted. "Olivia!" He tried the door again, then picked up his foot and kicked at it with all his strength, knowing what he would find before he even saw her. Water rushed out onto the floor as Olivia lay in the bath, submerged, with an empty pill container on the sink beside it. He rushed over and pulled her out, laying her sideways on the floor.

Pure instinct took over as he hit her sharply on the back. She was utterly unresponsive. He rolled her onto her back, covered her nose, and tried to blow life back into her lungs. Nothing—he was too late. One, two, three deep breaths, then he desperately applied compressions on her chest until suddenly her body convulsed and she began coughing out water.

Max quickly covered her in towels to keep her warm. When her eyes fluttered open, they were so full of pain he found himself looking away. She curled into a ball and began to cry and shake like a small child.

"I will call the doctor," Max said.

"No, ah, no no . . ." her words eked out, barely audible.

"Just be still. Everything will be okay. I'm right here." Max waited for a few moments with her until she was calm. "I'll get you some clothes," he said gently into her ear, and then left, leaving the door partially open. The letter was on the bed. He snatched it up and read it, then stood for a moment shocked, trying to regain some composure. His mind raced. It was explainable. Mrs. Winston was anemic and had passed out in the bath. It was fortunate he'd been in the kitchen—a tragic accident averted. He stared at the letter in his hands. Not knowing what to do with it, he put it in the folds of her cookbook and placed it in the storage box. He numbly pulled some clothes from the cupboard to dress her and went back inside the bathroom.

chapter nineteen

1996

Vene stared mindlessly out the kitchen window waiting for the kettle to boil. It was a rainy, wet day, the kind of day where the gray color of the sky felt like a prelude to darkness the whole time. The house was cold. She was cold, even in her oversized wool sweater.

She picked some mint from the window box behind the sink. It was always a wonder how Max was able to grow fresh herbs all year round. She took a glass teapot from the shelf, put the leaves inside, and poured the boiling hot water on top, swirling it around with a spoon. She reached for her mother's loveliest silver tray out of the cupboard and added some local homemade honey, fresh from the village shop, a small bowl of lemon slices, and two Wedgwood china cups with saucers. These days, the only thing her mother seemed to really enjoy was fresh mint tea, and Vene found great pleasure in serving it.

Max entered. "Can I help you?"

"No, I've got it. Thanks."

"I was thinking we'd have chicken for lunch if you'd like to help," Max said.

"That's a very sweet offer, Max, especially since you know I'd probably ruin it."

"You learn by trying. That's how your mother did it."

"Yes. So it seems. I've been reading her cookbook, Max, the one you gave her. And then I found something the other day, something that was . . . very unexpected. And sad."

Max looked at her steadily.

"A letter," Vene went on. "Written to my dad. A terrible letter."

"Oh," Max said.

"It must have been written before they left Napa for London, way back when, before I was born. She was desperately unhappy."

"Yes."

"Why?"

Max began busying himself at the kitchen sink. "Max, talk to me," Vene implored. "I know you know what happened. Something awful must have occurred to make her want to kill herself."

"It was a difficult time for her, and leaving the estate wasn't her choice."

"Yes, I know that already," Vene said impatiently. "I got that part—Dad was overbearing and made her move, and she had to follow him and give up everything she found passion in. But something else happened to that woman in that cookbook. What was it, Max? I need to know. I need to understand."

Max shook his head, looking troubled.

"She's dying, Max. Please . . . was it that winemaker? Victor Viandanti? Is he the PO box? Is that who the package was for?"

"Now is hardly the time to get involved, Vene. It's too late."

"It's never too late," Vene snapped. "I'm going to find out what happened, Max." She took the tray of tea and left the kitchen.

Upstairs in her mother's room, she found her father reading in his chair by the window. Her mother was asleep. On the surface, a sweet tableau, but it didn't tell the real story. Vene knew that now. There was love between them, even if she didn't understand what kind, but it hadn't been enough. And after all her mother had surely gone through, it was impossibly sad to imagine her dying so unhappy.

"Dad. I didn't realize you were up here." The room was chilly. The draft seeping in through the window was always so welcoming during the heat of the summer but an annoyance in the winter. Her parents both loved the Victorian aspects of their home and refused to update even the smallest detail. That style was more important than efficiency was something they both agreed on. "Do you want a blanket for your legs? I made tea for me and Mom, but I can go down and get you a cup if you like?"

"No, no, I'm fine. I'll leave you to it."

"You don't have to go. I'll get another chair. Stay, Dad, honestly. She should wake soon. She needs to take her meds. It might be nice for the three of us to be together and chat when she wakes, don't you think? The nurse will be coming in a minute."

Her father spent long hours in their bedroom but almost always, she couldn't help noticing, while her mother slept. Two unhappy parents, she thought numbly, and she didn't really know either of them. It was time for the truth. She put the tray down with some determination, but almost immediately, as if sensing confrontation, her father got up and kissed her mother on the top of her head, smoothed her hair, and left. Disappointed, Vene pulled up a chair and watched her mother sleep. Her slim fingers, her shoulders, her perfect mouth. But her beauty was overshadowed, or so it had always seemed to Vene, by a judgmental, rigid personality. She remembered thinking how perfect her mother was when she was younger. How much she wanted to look like her. She'd been twenty-seven when she had Vene, nearly the same age as when Vene had Dani.

Vene poured out some tea and read. *Il talismano* was now discreetly kept in the dresser drawer in the bedroom. She had taken to reading it like a novel instead of a recipe book and read quietly aloud as she flipped through the pages:

Osso buco—this dish takes too long
and impresses too little.

Tartufo—you haven't lived if you haven't had tartufo.
Sinfully delicious, like everything in my life.

Remember to make these profiteroles with extra cream—
the explosion in our mouths was wild.

Beef stew—sensible. Use one more splash of red wine
than called for. Reliable meal when feeling unreliable.

Max forcing minestrone for the pregnancy—
hate all food but this. No cravings . . . no desires.
Nothing. I have nothing—and everything.
It hurts so much, I actually feel numb.

She closed the book and stared at her mother, trying to picture the young woman from these notes, sinful and wild. It surely had to do with another man. She looked so peaceful in her sleep. Vene spoke to her in a whisper, knowing she couldn't hear her but wishing it was a real conversation between mother and daughter.

"Tell me, Mom, tell me what was going on. You were so . . . open . . . back then, everything visceral. And then you got pregnant, and it all seemed to change. Why was your pregnancy so awful? Were you sick? Did I make you sick, like Dani made me? Did Dad make you so unhappy? Or was it something else . . . someone else?" She paused and adjusted her mother's blankets, not daring to touch her body. "Being pregnant makes you raw and vulnerable. You should see some of the women I work with. Everything laying open . . . and it also can push you to make insane choices . . . I read your letter. The one to Dad. Jesus, Mom, you lost all hope. Lost your way. Lost yourself. Like me . . . I made an insane choice. My abortion—the worst decision of my life."

She got up, regret getting the better of her. Vene raised her hand to the window, and the glass panes were freezing to the touch. She recoiled. Just like her mother's heart, she instinctively thought, cold. Always reserved, controlled and private. Except now she knew better. There had been a free spirit in there once, a woman who cooked with abandon, a woman capable of such enormous emotion that she had tried to take her own life. Olivia had given Vene everything, a privileged background, a good education, everything but the things that really mattered: warm love, acceptance, the truth. She wanted badly to understand her mother, to forgive her. But every time she tried, she wrestled with the overriding emotion that welled up in her—resentment. And there was no escaping how sharp that felt.

There was a knock at the door. Vene wiped the tears from her eyes. "Come in."

The door opened and Jenny stood at the threshold. Vene looked at her, perplexed. Jenny returned the look with a compassionate smile.

"Hello, Vene. Can I come in?"

"Of course." Vene offered her chair and Jenny seemed comfortable to sit down, even though Olivia was asleep.

"Would you like some tea? It's fresh mint," Vene whispered, not sure of what to say or why Jenny was here.

"Oh no, I'm fine."

"I'm happy to go and get another cup—please, have some," Vene insisted, pouring a cup and setting it out for her. "Honey?"

"Sure, thank you."

Olivia began to stir. They both looked at her and waited. After a minute or so, her eyes opened, unseeingly. Vene put her face close to her mother's and spoke softly into her ear.

"Hi, Mom. It's about four o'clock. Jenny is here. I've made some fresh tea, and it's nearly time for your medicine."

Her mother sat up slowly. Vene tried to fluff up the pillows behind her head, but she immediately got annoyed.

"I've got it, please don't," she said, brushing Vene's hands away. Vene felt embarrassed in front of Jenny. But if Jenny noticed, she didn't let on. Vene poured her mother's tea and handed it to her.

"Shall I get some biscuits? Are you hungry at all?"

"No."

"Jenny?"

"No, thank you, Vene. I feel badly that I've taken your cup. Why don't I go and get another?"

"Don't be silly. I'll go down in a minute." Vene was more than intrigued by Jenny's presence in the room. What did her father's secretary want to talk to her mother about? It was quite something that she'd come into this room in the first place. Had she really had an affair with her dad? And if so, had her mother known? Cared even? Had her mother had her own affair? These two women in front of her were from a different era. The formality was stifling to Vene, and yet they both looked so relaxed in each other's presence—as if they knew and would stick to the role they were supposed to play. Vene turned on a few bedside lamps. For a woman who always had her "face" on with just enough makeup, it was odd to see Olivia look so bare in front of company. Vene had gotten used to the rawness of her mother's appearance, but Jenny? As if on cue, Olivia made an attempt to fix her hair.

"Thank you for coming up to my room. Apologies for not being able to see you downstairs."

"Of course."

"You've been so loyal, Jenny," Olivia said. "So very, very loyal," she added softly.

"As loyal as you," Jenny replied.

"Quite." Olivia allowed the moment to linger and took a sip of tea. "You've been with us from the beginning. Jonathan's whole professional career, right by his side."

"It's been a journey, to be sure."

"And now here we are."

"Yes."

"He's not always an easy man . . ."

"No, no, he's not," Jenny agreed with a small laugh.

"And he's not always a helpful man . . ."

"No, I can see that he's not."

"But he's a good man. Fair and kind."

"Yes, yes, I agree. And devoted too," Jenny added, looking right at her.

"Thank you for coming to visit. Jonathan said you've been several times. I'm afraid I've been very tired and not very good company."

"Anything I can do . . ."

"No, no, you've always done enough. I just wanted to say . . . well, take good care of him, Jenny. He will need your friendship, and he's not always good at asking for it."

"I understand."

"Yes," Olivia said. "Yes, I'm sure you do."

There was no animosity or resentment. A world of understanding lay between the two women, a common bond of loyalty for the same man all these years. Olivia's eyes drifted shut again, and Jenny stood to take her leave. They would probably never see each other again. But whatever acceptance Jenny had been looking for, it was clear to Vene that she had been given it.

"God bless, Olivia. Rest well." Jenny left the room, shutting the door gently behind her.

1946

Another cold dawn. Another day beginning. The colors in the sky were explosive. Pink, orange, brilliant crisp blue. Olivia sat on the ground, high on the hill, digging her fingers into the soil, her body too heavy to move. These were the vines that Victor had planted. She was waiting for something, some feeling, something to lift inside of her to allow her to get up and move on. She barely noticed Jonathan coming to stand next to her. He watched the sunrise for a moment, his hands buried deep inside the pockets of his wool trousers.

"Best part of December's shorter days," he finally said.

"What is?"

"Being able to catch the sunrise every morning."

Olivia nodded.

"Glad you're feeling better." Then, when she didn't respond, he added, "You must be chilly. You should come in. We leave in a few hours."

"I'll be there in a minute." She couldn't look at him.

"We'll be back. At some point we will come back, and you'll see, it will all be the same."

"It will never be the same."

"Well, no, we will have a family by then."

"That's not what I mean," Olivia said, knowing Jonathan wouldn't have a clue what she was talking about, not that she cared.

"Life is about choices, Olivia. Our choice to go abroad will be lucrative in more ways than you or I can imagine right now. Not many people have the president's ear. There will be another election, and then who knows where we will end up."

"It doesn't matter."

"What doesn't matter?"

"Where we end up. It doesn't matter where we end up because life here is over. I will stand by you, Jonathan, and I know you will stand by me and this child, and in the end, it doesn't matter where we live anymore."

"This baby is all you wanted. The rest is inconsequential. We will make it work wherever we are."

She got up from the ground.

"Thank you for your loyalty, Olivia. You won't regret it."

"Loyalty?" She laughed slightly. "I'm not loyal, Jonathan. I'm resolutely defeated," she said, and walked away. Ever since Max found her in the bathtub, Olivia had changed. There was harshness in her face, in her eyes. The loss of the new life she'd craved, no ending to this one. She walked inside the house. Stacks of boxes were being organized for shipping—their life being systematically emptied out of each room. All that remained were the paintings on the walls and the pieces of furniture too big to ship. Max was packing up the last of her precious wedding dishes in the kitchen.

Olivia noticed the care with which he was putting her beloved dishes away. His big, strong hands delicately wrapping tissue paper around each item. He had tried so hard to give her hope. The radio was on, and she could just make out the faint sound of a song she loved. How many nights had she and Max and Victor shared together, cooking and laughing and dancing? Next to the big box she saw her favorite tea bag dish, one of those small porcelain ones. Max knew she was particular about this small yet oddly meaningful item and had it in line to be wrapped as well. Care and thought went into everything he did for her, and she repaid him in that moment by being rude.

"Just leave them, Max. Don't bother. I won't be shipping any of this, so you can just leave everything where it is."

"But I've already packed away most of it, Mrs. Winston. The china dinner plates are the last pile."

"I don't want them," she replied.

"I suppose we can just store them downstairs. I presume you don't want anyone else using them while you're gone?"

"I really don't care, Max. You shouldn't either. Just put everything back on the shelves and busy yourself with something else." And with that, she left abruptly.

Survival, she kept telling herself. That's all she had to concentrate on now if she was going to build a new life abroad with a baby. A baby born out of her deepest love. A secret to be kept until the day she died. That burden was the punishment for her sins, or so she now believed. What kept her going was also a strange belief that guarding this secret was like honoring something sacred between her and Victor—their love forever kept alive in their child. It felt selfish and selfless all at once.

Olivia knew she had to tell Victor about the baby. She wrote him a letter, holding nothing back, declaring herself his forever. She vowed to write to him every year, on their child's birthday, expecting nothing in return. Another burden to bear. She sealed her letter with a kiss and then a golden-waxed circle with her initials imprinted on it. It was time to leave the estate, leave Napa, and leave the most intimate part of herself forever behind.

The staff rushed around downstairs making final arrangements with their luggage and boxes. Jonathan was outside giving instructions to the driver. He seemed emotionless about leaving. Of course he was, she thought. He was not capable of feeling anything.

Max stood by the entry holding her coat and hat.

She went to him, the only person in the world who could understand her pain. Her heart. She felt like a trapped animal. She put a hand on her abdomen as the tears started to fall. All she had ever wanted was a baby; for so long she'd prayed to get pregnant, to feel whole and normal and feminine, to define her life and give it purpose. And now . . . now it felt like a slow death sentence.

"Max—I'm sorry about earlier. I didn't mean . . ."

"It's no problem, Mrs. Winston. I'm sorry you're leaving too."

Olivia took the letter from her purse. "I need you to do something for me."

"Of course, whatever you need."

She leaned into him and whispered in his ear. "Find him, Max. Find out where he is, his vineyard or wherever, and mail this letter to him."

"But . . ."

"You must do this for me. Please," she implored. Somehow all the Italian people she knew were only a few degrees of separation from one another. She believed he would find him. And perhaps in the universe where everything felt right, he would find her and rescue her once more.

"Yes, Mrs. Winston." He looked into her eyes, then away after a glance at her belly.

Olivia threw her arms around him and hugged him. The other members of the staff stared for a moment. A break of protocol, to say the least. Max kept his arms by his side, but she held on for an extra beat before letting go. She touched his face with her hand as tears fell down her cheeks. "Thank you. For everything, dear friend, always. *Grazie*."

chapter twenty

1996

Four a.m. and quiet. No noise of wind or weather, no creaks or humming machines on standby. No movement of any kind throughout the house. Only the grandfather clock in the hallway with its dull tick marking the infinite passage of time. Vene was in a deep sleep when she suddenly awoke, startled. She grabbed her chest and tried to breathe but found herself crying and unable to control herself. "Oh my God, my God. Mom!"

In a daze, she raced out of bed and down the hallway, throwing open the door to her mother's room. A nurse stood over Olivia, and Vene gasped and froze.

"Is she dead? Did she die? I dreamt she died. Oh my God, Mommy, Mommy, can you hear me?"

The nurse held Vene back. "She's not dead," she whispered. "She's not dead, Vene. Calm down. It's all right. I just unplugged her machines for a while. That's all. The tubes were irritating her skin. I'm checking on her myself. She's peacefully sleeping, don't worry."

"I thought she was gone." Vene couldn't stop crying. "I must have just been dreaming. It was so real. What time is it?"

"Not even dawn. And you were up late with her reading. You've only been sleeping for a little while. She's completely fine. Go back to bed. Nothing is going to change, I promise. Go."

But Vene couldn't go. Anxiety and fear from an all-too-real dream still gripped her, and her only relief was to be by her mother's side. She stared at her. Dying stole from a person, bit by bit, until it left only a beating heart, breaths in and out, the simple bodily rhythms of existence. The morphine dose was already at 5 mg every four to six hours. Eventually that would go up to 10 mg around the clock, topped up with rescue doses for extended pain. The doctor had checked in on her a few days ago and things were stable, but he warned that the next stage would be the last. Jonathan had asked about how they would know when they were there, and the doctor told them that they would know, that the body would slowly shut down. They weren't there yet, but regardless the idea was to keep her as comfortable as possible.

In the stillness of early morning, Vene wrestled with her feelings. Here was her mother, the one person who repeatedly pushed all her buttons for reasons Vene had never understood. She knew her mother only had the power of control that she herself chose to give her, so why was it so hard to take that power back? She had always wanted to love her mother unconditionally, be loved by her unconditionally—the way she loved Dani, the way she loved her dad. But her mother created stumbling blocks she couldn't hurdle. Vene watched her breathing; it was slow and methodical until it seemed as if she was holding her breath—pause—nothing—and then a sharp inhale again. She wondered if her mother felt scared.

She climbed up onto the end of her bed and saw that her mother had been looking through her *Il talismano* cookbook. Vene held the book close and smelled it—its oil stains and dried flowers, crumbs and odd spices stuck between the pages alongside a world of secrets. "Oh, Mommy. Don't go yet," she whispered. "Don't leave me. Please. I'm not ready. You're not ready. Please.

Let me help you." Distraught, she stroked her mother's hair, tears rolling down her cheeks. Their vulnerability was intertwined—this she knew. Perhaps had always known.

Early the next morning, Max entered with a faint knock. Vene was already up and taking a shower while Olivia rested in bed. Max had a tray of mint tea with honey and lemon for Olivia and a fresh Italian coffee press for Vene. He set it down on the table. He was an old man now, moving more slowly, and what was left of his hair was white. He never spent a day working where he wasn't dressed formally in black trousers, a crisp white button-down shirt, and either a black vest or a white chef's jacket on top. The continuity of his uniform was comforting to everyone.

He looked over at Olivia, and she smiled back at him. No words were exchanged between them for some time; there often didn't need to be.

Finally, Olivia spoke. Her voice was soft and quiet. "She . . . Vene's everything I should have been."

Max smiled.

"I can't do it anymore, Max. I never really could. And now I'm tired . . . just so tired."

"It's the cancer. It takes all your energy away."

"It's not just the cancer. I'm empty. It's no one's fault. I blame myself. And everyone around me suffered because of it."

"That's not true, Mrs. Winston," Max protested.

"Oh, but it is. You know only too well how right I am. I paid for my sins, Max. Believe me, I paid."

"*Nessuno può prendere quello che è destinato a te.*"

"Which means?"

"No one can take the one that is destined for you."

"He *was* meant for me. I know. If I'm honest, I never realized when he left me that night, all those years ago, that I would never love again. To know what love is, really and truly have it, taste it—ha!—all that cooking . . . is to also know when it is *not* that."

Max could only nod. And then he said, "She was also destined for you. Vene. She was meant to be for you as well."

"Vene was my chance at happiness. She needed me so much at first. Her life depended on mine. Remember? I did feel that pure love again. Different of course, but powerful. And I felt . . . light. But then so quickly, Max, she started to grow up and push me away, even at such a young age. It's as if she knew something was wrong and didn't want to need me . . . love me. She didn't even want a cuddle. And who could blame her? Surely, I had no right. No right to stop her natural disdain for all that I had done." She paused—the memory still haunted her. "There was never going to be a happy ending for me, Max, was there?"

He was at a loss for an answer.

"I didn't do anything well," Olivia said.

"You learned how to cook . . ."

She laughed out loud. "Yes, you're right. I know how to cook. Best pomodoro this side of the valley."

"So said even my mother," Max added.

"Now that's a compliment. Learned from the pro."

"She died from high cholesterol. So did my father. I think she might have killed him."

Olivia was caught between a laugh and a cough. "That's not funny," she gasped.

Vene came into the room. "You okay? Mom, are you okay?"

Olivia settled herself. "Yes, I'm fine. Max was just reminding me about his parents' love for one another."

Vene looked to Max curiously. He smiled back, discreet as ever. The doorbell rang, startling all three of them.

"That's early," Olivia said.

"I'll get it," Vene replied, and shot downstairs.

Early morning sun spilled into the hallway. It was going to be a beautiful day. As Vene reached the bottom stair, her father came out of his study.

"Morning, my love."

"Morning, Dad. Did you sleep in there?"

"No, not exactly. I got up very early. Couldn't sleep, so I came down here."

The doorbell sounded again. They looked at each other.

"Are you expecting someone?" Vene asked. For some time now, neighbors had been rotating in, but word must have circulated that Olivia's condition had deteriorated because for the last few days everyone had kept their distance.

"No. I thought you must be."

Vene opened the door. Standing before them, leaning on a mahogany cane, was a man in a dark blue wool overcoat, a dark blue suit with a silk handkerchief, a crisp white shirt, and a panama hat. He looked elegant and distinguished and very foreign. Jonathan stared at him for a long moment without surprise. "Victor . . ."

"Mr. Ambassador," Victor said, taking off his hat and extending his hand.

The two men shook hands. Vene stood there, transfixed. *He had come!* She had called him and now he was here, and, well, he was far more handsome than she'd expected.

Jonathan put his arm around Vene. "Victor, this is my daughter, Vene. Vene, this is Victor Viandanti."

"Our infamous winemaker," she said, smiling charmingly, determined to give nothing away.

Victor smiled back. "Pleasure to meet you, Venerdi."

"Yes, Venerdi. Not many people get the Italian reference—but please, call me Vene."

"Vene," Victor repeated.

It took a moment before Jonathan said, "Please, come in."

"Let me take your coat," Vene said. Victor entered, giving her his coat and hat. "Some hat."

"*Grazie*," Victor replied, dipping his head ever so slightly.

The air was thick with something she couldn't quite detect. Vene had never seen her father so unsure of his manners. Vene had made a decision for her mother, and she was sure there was only something to gain by Victor coming. Whatever had transpired between him and her mother must have truly been something special to get an old man on a plane that quickly, but she hadn't thought about what it might mean for her father.

"Can I get you something to drink, or eat?" Vene asked hastily. "It's so early, and well, perhaps a coffee?"

"No, no. My apologies for coming without ringing first. My flight landed last night, and I drove up to the valley first thing."

"That's absolutely fine—right, Dad? Completely fine."

"Yes," Jonathan added reservedly.

"Is it nice to be back?" Vene asked awkwardly.

"I'm sure Mr. Viandanti is here to see your mother, Vene," Jonathan pointed out. "Perhaps you should take him up."

"Oh yes, sorry, of course!" Vene said. "I'll just hang up your stuff real quick." She took his coat and hung it up in the hallway closet.

Jonathan looked at Victor thoughtfully. "How did you know?" he asked.

"I received word."

"Ah." There was a beat. Then Jonathan added, "Your timing is . . . well, it isn't ideal. She's quite weak and not often awake for long."

"I see."

The two men fell into silence. Fifty years had passed since they were opposite one another and in this moment, Vene thought they both looked defeated. There was a noise on the stairs, and Victor looked up.

"Max," he said with a big smile.

If Max was surprised at the arrival of the old winemaker after so long, he didn't show it. "Mr. Viandanti," Max said, returning the smile. He offered his hand to shake, but Victor ignored it and embraced him warmly. Vene watched as Max allowed himself to be hugged, painfully aware that Jonathan was watching his every move, noticing their intimacy.

"Max," Jonathan started, "is my wife awake?"

"Yes, Mr. Winston."

"Well then, please show Mr. Viandanti upstairs to our bedroom."

"Yes, Mr. Winston."

As they walked upstairs, Jonathan went straight into his study and abruptly shut the door without saying a word to Vene. She stood in the hallway, unsure whether to go after him. He was upset, whether with her or Victor, she didn't know. But still . . . *Victor came*, she thought to herself, *he actually came*.

"Coffee?" Max offered, coming back down the stairs.

"Sure." Vene followed him into the kitchen.

"Why did you call him?" Max asked as they waited for the water to boil.

"Do you think I did the right thing? My dad sure as heck didn't look pleased."

Max poured the boiling water into the cafetiere.

"Max, tell me I did the right thing. Why else would she have written to him just before she dies? I mean, she obviously wanted to see him. She's been ticking boxes since I got here. I just wanted to give her something, you know, personal. I think I've read one too many recipes about him, if I'm honest. I know they were about him, Max. I figured that much out. I thought I could at least reach out and let him know she was dying. That's all I did. And he actually came!"

Max stayed silent.

"Max . . . talk to me."

"Who's to say what anyone needs. But yes, if you're asking, I do think it was a good thing you called. I didn't do it—I couldn't. But you—yes, it's a good thing." Max poured Vene and himself a cup of coffee, and they drank in silence until he eventually left the kitchen.

Jonathan was still in his study with the door closed, so Vene ventured upstairs. Outside her mother's room, she waited for a beat, conflicted. She was desperate to peer inside. She put her ear to the door, then knocked softly.

Victor was sitting with the chair pulled up to Olivia's bed. He had taken her hand gently in his and was holding it close to his heart. Her mother's face was completely relaxed, different than Vene had ever seen her. Her normally brittle expression was softened by her smile as she gazed at him. It was clear to Vene that she was staring at two people in love, and she marveled at the light between them.

"Mom . . ." she said finally.

Olivia looked up at her. "Vene!" She motioned for her to come closer. "Victor tells me you called him."

"Yes, Mom. I did."

"But how did you know to call?"

Vene looked at Victor. His eyes were wet with tears. Her mother was equally emotional. She decided to keep it simple. "The cookbook. It was all in there."

Olivia laughed. "Ah, my famous pomodoro . . . yes! Perfection in the end. I did get to perfection in the end, at least once."

Victor added, looking directly at Vene, "Yes, perfection at least once."

Vene's emotions were running awry. Bringing this man to her mother had been her only thought, but now, seeing them together, her father shut out downstairs, her mother's joy so obvious, she realized she'd reopened an old and complicated history.

"Thank you, Vene," Olivia said. "Thank you, thank you."

"You're welcome, Mom."

"He never would have come had you not asked." Olivia looked at Victor tenderly. Then she added, "He stayed away all these years out of love. I know that now . . . I always knew."

They'd been lovers, and then he left her. Vene could see it so clearly now. Her mother pining away for him, unable to find any real pleasure in life ever again. And yet, she thought, how instantly her mother had forgiven this man. Incredible. After all those years apart, they were two different people meeting now, yet not even their age seemed to dampen their chemistry. Suddenly, it felt intrusive to be in the room any longer. "I think I'll go."

Victor reached out his hand to her arm. "Stay, please. Just for a few moments."

Vene saw he was wearing a signet ring—a family crest design that she recognized. "Your ring, this design . . ."

"It is my family's crest."

Vene looked at her mother.

"It's on our label," Vene said.

Victor took off his ring and handed it to Vene.

"No," she said, embarrassed. "I don't want it. I was just admiring the design, that's all."

"Please, have it," Victor insisted.

"No, I couldn't."

"Vene . . ." Olivia started.

"Honestly, that's very kind, Mr. Viandanti, but I'd rather not."

"Of course," Victor said, putting the ring back on.

"Vene . . ." Olivia spoke up, "Victor came all this way . . ." Olivia looked at Victor, overwhelmed as tears filled her eyes, reaching for his hand once again.

Vene was in awe and resentful all in one breath. She knew that she could never fully appreciate the depth of feeling between this man and her mother, but she was used to not understanding her mother. She couldn't get swallowed up again by her inability to accept what was right in front of her. Truth be told, it was an odd relief, the knowing. An explanation for so much. It was clear her mother needed to be alone with him. She left the room and went back downstairs. Victor's coat and hat had been moved to the bench in the hallway—ready for his departure, it seemed. She guessed her father had put them there as a signal not to invite him to stay any longer. Vene picked up the hat and put it on her head, looking at herself in the hallway mirror. She set it back down and lifted up his coat, shaking off the dampness, and refolded it back on the bench. An envelope was sticking out of the inside pocket. She hesitated, glancing up the stairs to the mother's room, and then slid out a corner to find her mother's unmistakable gold-waxed seal. She thought it sentimental that he'd carried it all this way. It made her curious. She stared at it. It was completely wrong, and yet . . . there was so much she still didn't know.

My dearest Victor,

It's not Vene's birthday, but I'm taking what could be my last opportunity to write to you. For years—every year—on her birthday, I have written to you what was in my heart. I wanted to share with you what was also yours. After only hearing back just once after that first letter with your clearest desires and boundaries, I realized I never would send you a letter again. So I kept them instead. Our love would only be able to be explored in my dreams. This was a fate I would have to accept. My inability to leave all those years ago resulted in your never getting to know the beauty of Venerdi. I am sorry for so many things, but that part is the hardest. What we created together is spectacular—born out of a love that will never expire in me.

She is determined and idealistic, compassionate and full of resolve. She is loving and beautiful. She has been my greatest accomplishment and yet tied to my deepest sorrow, as watching her grow reminded me more and more of you. At times, the pain I feel when I look into her eyes is unbearable. I fear my unhappiness has let her down terribly. I hope my collection of letters tells the story of her life and soul justly. Jonathan has been an incredible father despite everything that's happened. We've never spoken about it and never will, and it really didn't matter to him, a diplomat to the end. Vene is his greatest joy. He loves her with all his heart.

It is very odd dying. Try as I might, I can't escape all the regret. As my own heart weakens in this life, know that it has always been yours.

Olivia x

Vene stood holding the letter for some time, shaking. Numbly, she went into the kitchen to find Max, but no one was there. How could her mother not have told her? How could she! She felt her anger start, and then grow. She stormed out of the house and headed to the cottage adjacent—Max's cottage.

"Max, Max . . . are you in there?" she called, banging on the door.

"Come in, Vene," she heard him say. She pushed inside to find Max lying down on his bed, resting, still in full uniform. His room was tidy as ever.

"He's my father? Are you kidding me?"

Max sat up. "He's your biological father," he said calmly, "not your real father."

"And that's supposed to make it okay? Why didn't they tell me?"

"I don't know."

"Why didn't *you* tell me?!"

"It wasn't my place, Vene."

"Jesus, Max . . ." She began to pace his room.

"When a decision is made like that in a family, the strength comes from each person's ability to accept where they are—and that's what they did," he explained.

"What about me? Do I get a second here to say *what about me*? This is insane! And so typical of my mother. She never once thought about how I would feel discovering this . . . this . . . new crazy reality!"

"You don't think she spent her whole life considering what was best for you? A father who prided himself on raising you versus a father who left?"

"So that's what happened? Victor just up and left when he found out I was on the way?"

"I don't know when he found out, but he didn't come back for you, no. For you or for her."

"Am I meant to feel sorry for her?" Vene said angrily.

Max remained calm. "They were very much in love. And it was a long, long time ago."

"This is all too weird and fucked up. And my father knows?"

"I'm sure he understands a lot."

"Oh God . . ." Vene felt the pang of what her father must have held inside all these years.

"I'm sorry, Vene. But your not being told, it was for the best."

"Really, Max? Was it?"

"You've been looking for the truth—well, here it is. But it doesn't always help, does it?"

Vene sat down on Max's bed, defeated. "I wanted to understand."

"I know," he said.

"And she stayed with my dad because of me, out of duty? How stupid is that?"

"She loves your father."

"Yeah, but not in the way she loves Victor. I saw the way they looked at each other just now. I wouldn't have stayed, Max—I wouldn't have."

"And you didn't."

"No, I didn't," Vene replied almost defiantly.

"But she did. And she tried to do the right thing, Vene. I can promise you that. She always loved you as best she could."

"Yeah, so she wrote," Vene said sarcastically.

"Not all your childhood was awful," Max replied pointedly.

"So, she wrote to him every year, and he only wrote back that once? Never called? Nothing?"

"No, I don't believe he did."

"All that time . . ."

Max paused with a memory. "She did try leaving once."

"What happened?"

"She got as far as the airport. She never took her bags out of the trunk. The next thing I knew, she was picking you up from your riding lesson and was home in time for dinner."

"God . . ."

"I won't say she did it all for you, but she certainly didn't live her life for herself—that much I know. It's hard for you to understand. You never waited for others to give you permission. Even when you were a young girl, you'd get an idea in your head and before anyone knew it, you'd jump into whatever it was that was in front of you without another thought."

"It's at least honest, even if you don't approve."

"It's who you are, Vene. It's just not who your mother is," Max explained.

"Yeah, well—the whole thing is tragic." Vene tried to calm down. She lay next to Max. He waited with her, not saying more. And then she felt the tears come. She had held herself together so tightly for so long. It was all too much. Max took her hand in his, lost too in his own sadness.

Vene lay there for some time, thoughts ricocheting from herself to her mother, to Victor. She couldn't have imagined that discovering who her mother really was would make her question her own identity. But maybe that was the point. It had always been easier to hold her mother accountable for their lack of connection—and her mother had taken it, accusations and all. The burden of her secrets clearly consumed her.

Vene looked around the room. It had been years since she was last in Max's room. Fifty years he'd lived here, at least for five days a week. She'd never asked where he went on his days off—assuming he stayed with some relative, another Italian living in the city somewhere. Some weeks, he wouldn't go at all. Max had always been there for her. He appeared in every childhood memory. She knew she would need him when her mother was gone. If nothing else, for all the good memories that told her story, along with the bad ones—a rewrite in places, but that was normal.

She returned to the house a while later and was surprised to find Victor in the hallway, putting on his coat. His eyes looked very sad. Max appeared from the kitchen and handed Victor his hat. Victor touched Max's shoulder tenderly before turning back to Vene.

"You're leaving," she blurted out.

"Yes."

"My mother was very happy to see you."

"As was I. I waited a long time to see her . . . to meet you."

She could sense his awkwardness, but again she felt her resentment rising. *How could you have left her for so long? Broken her heart so deeply?*

"Oh . . . yes. It's a lot to take in. So much to think about." She searched his face. Did they have the same features? His eyes were brown like hers, his hair was thick . . .

"Yes. I understand," Victor said.

"Do you plan to stay in Napa for a while, or are you going back to Italy?"

"I'm here for the next few days only."

"I see," Vene said.

"Have you ever been to Italy?"

"No, never. I've always wanted to go, though. It looks beautiful."

"It is," Victor replied. "You should come and see for yourself."

"One day, I'm sure I'll get there."

"I could show you Tuscany if you would like."

Vene tried to keep her composure. *Bit late now, surely—now that all is revealed, and my mother is nearly gone. Where were you all this time*? But she also didn't want her anger and confusion to shut the door on him forever.

"My husband is Italian," was what came out.

"Ah, yes. From where?"

"He left as a baby, outside of Milan, a small village. He still has family there . . . distant relatives, but still. We've talked about going many times. Maybe I'll go with him."

"Good, good. Italy is not so big, but there is a lot to see. To discover."

"My mother always wanted to go," Vene said, unable to keep the accusation out of her voice. But there was unmistakable sorrow attached to the comment as well, and it was a loss they both recognized.

"Yes. I know."

"Goodbye, Mr. Viandanti." She composed a smile. "Until next time."

"I hope so, Venerdi. Goodbye."

"Well, then . . ." She opened the door.

Victor stood in front of her, and time suspended. He reached up to her face and held it gently in his hands. Vene remained still, unexpectedly caught up in the tenderness of his touch.

"*Tesoro, Venerdi. Sei un angelo.*" He kissed the top of her head.

"*Grazie, Mr. Viandanti. Vorrei essere stato.*" And she did wish she were an angel, because an angel would forgive much more easily. Victor Viandanti was a stranger to her; her mother had made it that way. But she had found the truth, and she knew it was up to her to reconcile herself to it.

Just then, she realized her father was watching them from the threshold of his study. Vene looked between him and Victor as the two men faced each other silently. Vene moved to her father and put her arm around his waist.

"Goodbye, Mr. Viandanti," she said softly.

"Ciao," Victor said, tipping his hat to Jonathan as the door shut behind him.

chapter twenty-one

1996

It was a cold day in Napa. It had snowed the night before, and the mountains overlooking the valley below were sprinkled in white. The clouds lay low and heavy, dark gray puffs above the hills. The vines were barren, the trees like charcoal sticks. The road leading up to Tulocay Cemetery was so full of cars that people had to park a quarter of a mile away and walk.

Napa's royalty had turned out to say goodbye to Olivia. All the giants of the wine industry had come to pay their respects. It was a world Jonathan had always believed himself on the outside of, and yet here they all were, reverent and supportive.

Vene, Dani, Tony, and Jonathan traveled together in the first limousine behind the hearse, with Max and Jonathan's two sisters—who had flown in the day before—following in another. The remaining staff drove behind, part of a long procession of cars.

The hearse stopped and Dani grabbed Vene's hand. She looked at her mom, her eyes red and sad. Not much had been said between any of them in the last few days following Olivia's death. She had passed quickly and peacefully by herself in the early hours of the morning. When Vene woke to the news, it hadn't come as a surprise that her mother died alone. She'd known that when Victor left, there would be nothing else to live for.

Inside the chapel, a sole violinist was playing "Hallelujah" as the family followed the coffin inside. It was Jonathan's favorite song and one of the few choices he made for the service. Vene looked around at all the familiar faces. Even Robert had showed up, making sure to give Dani a loving hug as she passed—and trying unsuccessfully to catch Vene's eye. Everyone wanted to share in their pain. And it was pain Vene was feeling. To be standing there with her own broken heart was something she hadn't expected. She'd been so focused on reconciliation, she'd forgotten about loss.

The immediate family took a seat in the reserved front row, Vene sitting between Jonathan and Dani. She could feel her father trembling, age and emotion finally getting the better of him. Her dad would never fall apart, though; it wasn't his style. As for Vene, everything she'd learned over the last few weeks needed to be felt, absorbed, come to terms with, slowly. This was not the time. Dani needed her to be strong. As Father Mark began the service, they relaxed a little, allowing religion to take over the formalities. Vene looked around. She caught sight of Fi sitting next to another childhood friend, Andrea, who'd never left Napa. It was funny who left and who didn't. Every pew was full—locals, friends, the wine community, and staff from the estate. It was oddly tender to see Pedro and his wife and four young children all dressed up in their Sunday best to pay their respects. Olivia's passing had resonated throughout the community, and that, Vene thought wryly, was something her mother would have enjoyed.

"The Lord is my shepherd; I shall not want . . ." Vene turned to Max, who was sitting behind them. He looked sad and tired, but then he'd lost a good friend in a great battle. She touched his arm, herself comforted by having him so close. Max touched her hand in response and smiled. Jenny was sitting directly behind

Jonathan. Of course, thought Vene. She was the woman who had been waiting behind him forever. Next to her sat Tony, radiating love and support, as always. He never did stand a chance with her mother—Tony the Trigger, Vene now thought of him. How many times her mother must have looked at him as "the other choice," the other path she herself could have followed. "All Things Bright and Beautiful" was being sung, followed by "Ave Maria" played by a violinist. Vene thought the selections generic. She regretted not taking the time to choose something more special—another missed opportunity. She'd tried, she would tell herself later, in every way she had tried in the end to be a good daughter.

Father Mark had begun his address. He spoke of Olivia's innovative efforts in gardening during times of trouble in their country, how she'd championed the cause of giving food to the needy. How she'd helped put Napa on the map with local artists, of her work fundraising for the Napa Valley Museum for the last twenty years. He described her love of the winery and a life well lived, before moving on to her family. Here was a woman who'd had it all, he seemed to be saying, a thriving wine label, an adoring husband, daughter, and granddaughter. A picture book story presented for the afterlife, Vene thought. Perception was everything. What did someone really know about another? All those years, what had Vene really known about her mother?

Jonathan pushed himself to his feet. Vene had been unsure whether he'd feel up to it, but her father was an orator, after all, and knew how to rise to an occasion. "On behalf of my family, I would like to thank you all for being here." He looked slowly around the room from behind the podium, his hands shaking slightly. "It's fair to say Olivia would have been overwhelmed with the wonderful attendance today. My wife and I were married for over fifty years. We met during a time when our world was at war. When fear and anxiety overwhelmed many. Just about the last thing on this diplomat's mind was love. But one evening, there she was, a woman with hope and sunlight in her eyes, and I just couldn't look away. She was mesmerizing. As my friend Winston Churchill once said of himself, 'My most brilliant achievement was my ability to persuade my wife to marry me.' I would hasten to agree."

As Jonathan continued on, Vene's mind wandered back to her last moments with her mother. Victor had left, Jonathan had retreated once again to his study, and she'd found herself alone, blindsided by all that had been revealed. She went into her mother's room and sat close to her bed, watching her sleep for some time. The heart monitor—which had been turned off during Victor's stay—was now back on, beeping quietly. The nurse left the room so they could be alone.

"Is he gone?" Olivia finally whispered, blinking her eyes open.

"Yes, Mom, he left a little while ago."

Olivia looked at her daughter and slowly took Vene's hand in her own. Vene couldn't remember the last time she'd held her mother's hand. Her instinct was to punish her mother for the madness of all she now knew, but instead she held on.

"Good. It's better he's gone now. It would upset your father otherwise."

"My father . . ." Vene replied.

Olivia shook her head and began caressing Vene's hand as she held it. "Oh, Vene . . . I'm so sorry. So very sorry."

Vene's eyes filled with tears. She felt torn—wanting the connection, the honesty, but the reality of it brought unexpected heartbreak.

Olivia continued, "There was a world, an entirely different world where I once lived . . . where you were conceived. It was a Friday, after all."

"And he never tried to come back? How could you forgive him for leaving you? Leaving us?"

"Victor is an all-or-nothing kind of man," Olivia explained. "He wanted us to join him in Italy. Wrote to me to tell me so. His arms were open—but only if he could have us fully. He was never interested in being the 'other' man in my life and wouldn't compromise on that."

"Oh, Mom . . . so many secrets. Your life, and mine too, made from so many secrets."

"You have every right to see it that way."

"Is there another way to see it?" Vene asked. "I'm trying to understand your past as it actually was, to ease my mind, to forgive you. But it's not that easy."

The dagger thrown, finally. "Forgiveness. Yes, I suppose that is what I'm after in the end. That is what's needed . . . I know it's hard to imagine, but there weren't a lot of options at the time. I tried not to risk your happiness for mine."

"You made a decision I never could have. Who knows if it was the right one? I guess I'm sorry for you . . . and this, now, this isn't easy for me." The two women sat together, holding hands, trying to find some peace between them until Olivia softly closed her eyes, releasing her own tears.

"Sleep now, Mom." Vene leaned forward and gently kissed her mother's cheek. "Time to sleep."

Up on the podium, Jonathan was just finishing. "Our land in Napa is strong because of her. Our family is strong because of her, and my life will forever be enriched because of her. God rest her soul."

Father Mark put his hand on Jonathan's arm. Jonathan sat down, his shoulders heavy. Vene reached over and gave her father's hand a squeeze. He looked so old. Their relationship had always been so simple, and she never wanted to change that. It wasn't worth the risk. And it didn't matter anyway—not to her at least, and he had proved it didn't matter to him either. How impossible it would have been to imagine when she'd come home all those weeks ago that her life would take such a different turn.

That all she thought was certain, wasn't. That all that she questioned would become clear. The choices her parents made and the commitment they shared for one another lasted their entire lifetimes. To her, it felt like settling. But to them, it was devotion. There must have been some sort of strength derived from that that fueled the rest—albeit not a lot of genuine happiness. She'd never given Robert a second thought once she was out the door. He wasn't a terrible option, but it was as if she hadn't even considered staying once she met Tony. How could she? Vene always lived her life without the need or desire for approval from anyone. Anyone except her mother.

The service concluded with the final prayer from Father Mark. Mourners began to file out of the chapel. Vene walked straight outside to the fresh air, unable to breathe. She felt her grief like a mass of pressure expanding inside her chest. She put her hand on her heart involuntarily to hold it in place, suddenly desperate to be alone. She climbed straight into the limo and slouched in the back, anxiously awaiting her family but knowing they would be shaking hands and accepting greetings for a while before leaving for the estate. She saw one of the chambermaids and quickly climbed out of the limo.

"Stella, do me a favor?" she said, her voice barely audible. "Please, can I drive your car back to the house and you can go in the limo?"

"With Mr. Winston?" the girl asked fearfully.

"Yes, it's fine. Please . . ." Vene replied desperately.

Max walked up. "What do you need, Vene?"

"I need to get out of here, Max. Right now. Stella can go with my dad and Tony and Dani."

"I'll take care of Stella," Max said, motioning for Stella to give her the keys. Vene got into the beat-up Camaro, wrenched at the gearbox, and sped off.

She approached their gravel driveway and took the right turn hard and fast. It was the first time she had driven back to the house without her mother waiting inside. As she reached the top of the drive, she looked up at the master bedroom window. Even though the sun shone bright, the curtains were drawn. A flag being flown at half-mast, she thought. Everything was already changing. She drove the car to the back and parked it in the staff parking. The caterers were coming in and out of the house. Vene swapped her heels for outdoor boots and walked up onto the hillside behind, unable to face anyone just yet. She sat down for a long while by the Italian grapes, planted so long ago, and stared out over the meadows.

A sea of bright blue butterflies fluttered past—maybe a hundred of them, moving together effortlessly in the wind, as though performing a magic act. She wondered if her mother had ever felt the freedom of a butterfly's dance. All her thoughts and memories seemed to suddenly swirl around with them. Her mother had lived so much of her life with regret. Too much. And just then the butterflies dispersed, and Vene felt poleaxed by her loss. Tears streamed down her cheeks. Lost in what had been and no longer was. Lost in her own world of loving and hating. Lost, without her mother.

"Mom?" She heard Dani's voice from somewhere. "Mom? You up there? Everyone is starting to arrive, and we need you."

"Coming," she said. "I'm coming." She stood up, wiping the tears from her face. She looked once more out amongst the valley, the vines, and then slowly made her way down to the house.

epilogue

"What made you choose Italy?" asked the young woman sitting in the seat next to Vene.

"I have family there," Vene replied.

"Wow, that's cool. My boyfriend is Italian. I'm moving there myself. My mom thinks I'm crazy, but that's nothing new. Guess I'll see if I really like it, right?"

"Sure. It's the only way."

"Yeah. The only way to really know, right? I'm twenty-seven, so it's about time I decided to go for it."

"Twenty-seven. Good age." Vene had to laugh at the irony of her age. She looked out the window of the plane, taking in the rolling hills, the old buildings. Life was about choices, she thought. At any moment, any single decision could dictate the rest of your days. At twenty-seven, Olivia had made a choice out of honor and devotion, forever saying goodbye to love. There hadn't been much freedom fifty years ago for a woman to live a life less ordinary. The real tragedy, Vene knew, was that she was on this plane and not her mother.

She had always hoped that there was something more to her relationship with her mother than stupid quarrels. She knew that every story had many sides, and yet she'd never bothered to look deeper. She wished she had done so sooner. Understood sooner. If Vene could talk to Olivia's twenty-seven-year-old self, she would tell her to get on that plane and find Victor, to follow her heart, no matter what would have become of her daughter. And there in that moment, in thinking that, she felt all that her mother had given up, all that she'd tried to provide, sacrificing her own heart. And she suddenly realized she'd found what she'd been looking for all those years. It was more than reconciliation or forgiveness. It was gratitude.

The view outside the plane's window was beautiful. Her mother would have loved it. The vineyards, the olive trees, the colors of Italy would have fed her soul. Vene thought of Dani and her desire to share this new journey; there would be time for that, she'd make sure. She thought of Tony and the relief she felt for having met him, her own life taking that turn. And then she thought of Victor, and what it was going to be like seeing this country through his eyes, seeing the life he created there—meeting family she never knew existed. It was a path her mother had laid out for her a half a century ago, and it was finally time to follow it.

acknowledgments

Writing a novel is like climbing a steep mountain; the only way to finish is to put one foot in front of the other until you get to the top. I must say, the view is worth it. This endeavor was made possible by the love and guidance of many.

I'd like to thank my parents. I got lucky from the start with two incredible role models who gave their love unconditionally and energetically. They also gave me the best siblings anyone could wish for in Nathan, David, and Nancy, and then all of their families. It set me up for life.

My greater Hamm family and friends in LA and London make me feel grounded and supported regardless of where I am. A thousand times, thank you.

My early readers were essential to writing this book. They often read and reread. They provided insight and inspiration, giving me their time and their focus. Thank you so very, very much, Nancy Ross, Vivienne Vella, Lene Bausager, Valencia Haynes, Suzanne Warren, Helena Heyman, and Madrona Casey.

To Heather Jones, Sophie Matthews, Rebecca Frayn, and Rory Green, who went above and beyond, time and again, reading and thinking and designing with me. I'm grateful for your artistic talents and friendship. To Kim Raver, Jo Segal,

Gail Taylor, Keli Cela—walkie-talkies til my ideas were clear and strong. Thank you.

Thank you, Erika Rosenast, for editing the early stages with such care and intelligence. Thank you, Jen LaCorte, my resident Napa wine producer, whose knowledge, energy, and Promise rosé I always rely on.

Laura Hopper, thank you for sitting in front of me in high school English class. My writing has only improved because of you. Your energy and positivity kept me pushing on to find the right team, and I'm beyond grateful for your belief in me.

To Bella Pollen, my editor extraordinaire. You are a gift to any writer. Your clarity, voice, and understanding of prose and story elevated my words at every turn. Thank you for saying yes to this journey with me.

To Brooke Warner, Shannon Green, and the entire team at She Writes Press. You are strong, innovative, wise, and positive, and it is an honor for me to be a part of the SWP family. You have figured out a way to say "yes" to new talent when so many remain stuck with their "no." Thank you.

To Crystal Patriarche, Tabitha Bailey, and Grace Fell at Booksparks—your enthusiasm and guidance has encouraged me to find my feet and enjoy the ride.

To my four sons, my deep and true appreciation of what love is and its many layers comes from being your mom. I'm thankful for each of your lights in my life—that is what shines on and on within me.

To my beloved husband, Nick, whose artistry has inspired me to create my own, and whose love I depend on to walk forward in life. Hand in hand, always.

And finally to Kelly Hail, whose inspiration and creative genius at the inception of this project and these characters yielded the world in this book. Thank you for trusting me and for writing all over my cookbook one Sunday night in LA before family dinner. I wouldn't be here without you, and I hope I did you proud.